# Twilight of Honor

*A Military Wife's Story of the Healing Power of
Love Despite the Hardships of War*
*-The Vietnam Era and Its Aftermath-*

## Annie Laura Smith

**The Ardent Writer Press, LLC**
**Brownsboro, Alabama**

Visit Annie Laura Smith's
Author Page at

**www.ArdentWriterPress.com**

ISBN 978-1-938667-04-6

First Edition

## *Dedication*

Colonel James R. Kiser, USAF Retired,

and Margie B. Kiser

***

## *Acknowledgements*

With thanks to 1st Lt. Joseph W. Connaughton, USAF Veteran, and Major Mark E. Hubbs, USA Retired, for their historical and military guidance.

# CONTENTS - TWILIGHT OF HONOR

| | |
|---|---|
| *Prologue* | *1* |
| *Chapter One* | *3* |
| *Chapter Two* | 22 |
| *Chapter Three* | 42 |
| *Chapter Four* | 67 |
| *Chapter Five* | 85 |
| *Chapter Six* | 106 |
| *Chapter Seven* | 131 |
| *Chapter Eight* | 161 |
| *Chapter Nine* | 177 |
| *Chapter Ten* | 199 |
| *Chapter Eleven* | 220 |
| *Chapter Twelve* | 248 |
| *Chapter Thirteen* | 270 |
| *Epilogue* | 297 |
| *Author's Note* | 307 |
| *About the Author* | 308 |

## TWILIGHT OF HONOR
## PROLOGUE

MARCH 29, 1973 - A C-130 flew the last American combat contingent from Tan Son Nhut Airport in Saigon, but casualties and MIAs mounted until Saigon fell on April 30, 1975. The Vietnam War - a war which was never officially a war - was over on December 23, 1972, for Major Michael Reardon. He was first reported missing in action and later confirmed to be "killed in action, body not recovered" during a bombing mission of a strategic target on the North Vietnam border. His death occurred only six days before President Nixon halted the United States air offensive in North Vietnam. Major Reardon joined 58,000 other Americans who would not be coming home from Southeast Asia.

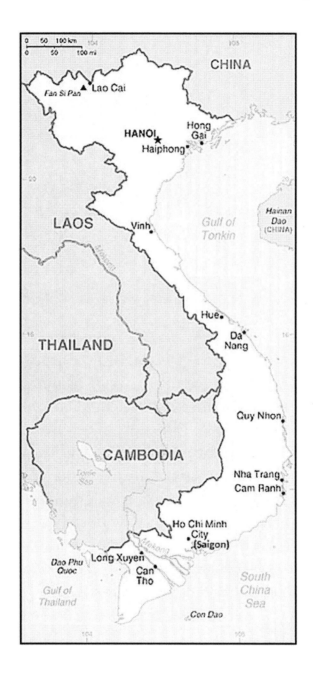

## *Chapter One*

*Sunday, April 29, 1973, Destin, Florida*

THE INVITATION READ "You are cordially invited to attend Shoreline Gallery's Open House, Sunday, April 29, 1973, 3:00 - 5:00 p.m.". Wynne Reardon was overwhelmed at the response to her Gallery's first Open House as guests mingled and chatted throughout the display areas, admiring the fiber art and pottery. She felt a vitality that had been absent for months as she moved among her friends renewing acquaintances, and explaining more about the different pieces. Their gaiety and laughter were an affirmation of her dream for the Gallery. It was finally a reality and from the number of people attending the Open House, the Gallery appeared to be well received.

"Wynne, it's your best work yet."

She turned to see her friend, Jean Stearns, admiring the large fiber art piece hanging on the cedar wall. The sunburst design in orange and yellow hues on the perfectly woven mandala brightened the entire corner of the room. The yarn fibers caught the waning sunlight streaming through the louvered windows.

"Oh, Jean. What else would a good friend say, but thank you...it was the most difficult piece I've ever done, but I'm pleased with it."

Wynne looked at the wall hanging with misty eyes. She had planned to give it to Michael for his study -- the colors were his favorite.

"And look at you!" Jean said, holding her friend at arm's length. "That dress is exquisite...I'm green with envy."

Wynne laughed and ran her hand over the fabric she had so carefully chosen for the occasion. The soft Egyptian cotton in emerald green complemented her auburn hair and hazel eyes. She had designed and made the dress especially to accentuate her trim figure. Her slim waist was belted with a self-made woven tapestry belt.

"See you later," Jean said with a quick hug.

Wynne nodded and turned to see an Air Force Major standing by her side.

"Now that's my kind of art." The distinguished looking gray-haired officer looked appraisingly at the work. "The colors...the textures...it's a magnificent combination..."

"Why, thank you. I'm Wynne Reardon. Welcome to Shoreline Gallery."

"Glenn Johnson. It's my pleasure."

She extended her hand, delighted with the compliment. But a numbing wave swept over her when she saw the cross above the officer's left shirt pocket. She felt again the paralyzing dread, and covered her face with her hands, momentarily turning away from the Chaplain's startled look. "Mrs. Reardon, are you all right?" the Chaplain asked as she regained her composure.

"I'm fine," she said, but unshed tears burned her throat. "About the piece...I sketched the idea while my husband and I were stationed in Hawaii. The sunsets there are unparalleled."

"Indeed they are," the Chaplain agreed. "It reminds me of the sunsets I often watched from Bellows Beach. I'm sure you must have gone there, too."

Memories of Hawaii and Bellows Beach were so real. Wynne could smell the heady and exotic fragrance of the Plumaria blossoms. They often hung their Plumaria leis in an open window, and the fragrance would waft through the room, even when the petals were brown.

"Yes, I did...that is we...excuse me please..." she managed to say, and fled from the room to the security of her office. The laughter echoing from her guests suddenly sounded strangely out of place as she shut the door to silence it.

*Would there ever be a time she could see a Chaplain without experiencing this searing panic? Would the pain always be there, ready to surface in even the most guarded times?*

Michael Reardon's face smiled up at her from his photograph on her desk. Those happy blue eyes and easy smile had always been there for her. Gently clutching the picture of her husband to her chest, she whispered, "Michael, I'm not sure I can make it."

Wynne did not hear the door open quietly behind her, nor sense her friend's presence until Jean slipped an arm around her shoulder.

"Oh, Wynne, please come back and join us for the Open House. Michael would want you to enjoy it."

Wynne nodded, wiped the tears from her cheeks, and returned to the main gallery with her friend to visit with the other guests.

\*\*\*

*Five Months Earlier - December, 1972*

ONLY FIVE MONTHS ago in early December Wynne had been jubilant -- Michael was finally finishing his tour as a fighter pilot in Vietnam. She had spent endless days and nights getting the Gallery ready to open before his return. No more working out of a studio at home. Shoreline Gallery was the culmination of her dream -- of their dream. But Michael was not entirely a dreamer -- he had insisted on an exhaustive feasibility market survey for the Gallery's location. The Destin area appeared to meet all of the criteria for success.

They had purchased an abandoned candy factory in Destin, a community in Florida's Panhandle, for a reasonable price. The bargain purchase had left enough funds to remodel, and decorate the interior into the rustic fiber art and pottery gallery she had always wanted. And now Michael would be home to share her joy. He would be stationed close by at Eglin Air Force Base for at least three years. This would be enough time to get the gallery established and find a director. Then it would be here when they were ready for retirement. Life was indeed full of promise for the Reardons. The long year of separation was nearly behind them, and the New Year held excitement and anticipation.

The news had been filled with reports of heavy U.S. bombing in Southeast Asia, and she had worried about Michael's safety.

"Don't worry," he had written. "I'm an experienced warrior...nearly enough missions to come home..."

In October Presidential Advisor Henry Kissinger and North Vietnamese negotiator Le Duc Tho had conducted cease-fire talks in Paris. President Nixon would surely announce an end to the war soon. Michael's homecoming would then be assured.

She tried to explain what was happening to their children, Stephen and Lauren, although their understanding at ages 11 and 9 was somewhat limited.

"Our President is trying to end the war," she told them one morning at breakfast, "so Daddy can come home soon."

"How can they do that?" asked Stephen with the inquisitive look that only an 11-year-old boy could have.

"Presidential Advisor Henry Kissinger is in Paris talking with officials from Vietnam," Wynne said.

"What's an official?" Lauren asked, her blue eyes staring at her mother.

"It's someone who represents the government of Vietnam," Wynne explained.

"Can he send Daddy home?" Lauren asked as she wiped milk from her mouth.

"Of course he can," Stephen said. "Officials make decisions!"

Wynne smiled at Stephen's authoritative tone. He had always tried to be older than his years.

"Stephen's right," Wynne agreed. "The official can decide to end the war so Daddy can come home."

"Yippie!" Lauren said, jumping up, and hugging her mother. Stephen shyly put his arm around his mother's waist, too.

\*\*\*

WYNNE WENT THROUGH the first two weeks of December in a state of euphoria. She worked diligently at the Gallery to put the finishing touches on the interior while trying to keep abreast of all of the news reports from Vietnam and Paris. Her spirits, too, were boosted by the headline in the morning paper on December 30th: PRESIDENT NIXON HALTS UNITED STATES AIR OFFENSIVE ACTION AGAINST NORTH VIETNAM ON DECEMBER 29th AS PEACE TALKS PROGRESS. Michael's homecoming was imminent!

\*\*\*

*Sunday, December 31, 1972*

THE DOORBELL AWAKENED Wynne from a deep sleep on Sunday morning. She glanced at the clock, and noted it was only 6:30 a.m. *Who could that possibly be at this hour, and on New Year's Eve?* She groggily reached for her robe. *Jean probably ran out of milk,* Wynne mused as she walked to the front door, expecting to see her best friend, who was also her neighbor.

When she opened the door, two uniformed Air Force Officers stood on the front porch in the yellow light of dawn. Behind them, a blue staff car loomed ominously in the driveway. Wynne's eyes were transfixed by the cross above the young 1st Lieutenant's shirt pocket.

"Mrs. Reardon I'm Colonel Rutledge," said the taller, graying man, the Squadron Group Commander at Eglin. "This is Chaplain John Turner. We have some news about Michael..."

Wynne felt her strength going, as hot and cold shivers of dread reverberated through her body. She had been a military wife long enough to know a Commander and Chaplain visiting at such an hour would carry bad news. *Not Michael!* she prayed silently.

Chaplain Turner reached for her arm to steady her.

"May we come in?" Colonel Rutledge asked.

"Oh, I'm sorry, please do."

Wynne led the men to the living room and sat on the sofa, dazed, suspended in uncertainty, afraid to know.

"Wynne, the news about Michael isn't the worst, but it's not good either...he had to eject during a mission over North Vietnam on December 23rd. His parachute was sighted going down in enemy territory. It was a vital mission...he was bombing a strategic target. We don't know any more at this time."

Wynne was too numb to reply. She sat mute, staring at the officers. *A vital mission? What was more vital than Michael coming home? The words missing in action* raced through her thoughts. *Not dead, but missing in action! Just missing. There was still hope.* Her vision blurred from tears as she reeled from the news. She couldn't see the officers' faces clearly, and the words *missing...missing...missing* echoed in her thoughts.

"Is there anything we can do for you...a friend we can call?" Chaplain Turner asked as he placed a hand gently on her shoulder. Wynne shook her head and managed to find her voice.

"When will you have more information?"

"We should have another intelligence report by tonight. We'll let you know," Colonel Rutledge replied. "There is a cease-fire in effect with the North Vietnamese," he added. "This will help in any rescue attempt since his parachute was sighted going down in enemy territory."

Yet Wynne knew his unspoken words were, "Rescue behind enemy lines was very hazardous."

"Thank you," Wynne whispered. The room seemed to whirl in a blur of tears.

"Let us call someone to be with you," Colonel Rutledge urged.

"Yes," Wynne mumbled. "Please call Jean Stearns. Her number is by the telephone in the kitchen."

Wynne heard Chaplain Turner's muted voice from the kitchen as he spoke on the telephone. He returned to the living room and said softly, "She'll be right over."

In a moment there was a knock on the door. When the Commander opened it, Jean rushed past him to her friend, embracing her.

"Michael's missing in action," Wynne said with a sob. "Missing..."

"He'll be all right...he'll be all right. Wynne, everything will be all right," Jean assured.

Wynne nodded, sobbing as Jean continued to embrace her.

Jean made coffee -- "Everything looks more positive after coffee." -- and the officers joined them at the kitchen table, asking gentle questions about family, former assignments, perfunctory questions one asks upon meeting new friends.

Wynne could only answer yes or no in a voice that didn't sound like her own. Jean filled in the details. They were like sisters, having known each other since their husbands' first tours of duty.

"We'll be going now," Colonel Rutledge said as he stood. "Here is the official report from the Casualty Office at Randolph." He handed the typewritten sheet to Wynne who took it, and followed the men to the door.

Chaplain Turner placed his hand on her shoulder. "Please call if we can be of any assistance."

"I will," she assured and closed the door. She then opened the letter that seemed heavier than anything she had ever held and read the message.

*Dear Mrs. Reardon:*

*It is with deep personal concern that I inform you your husband's plane was shot down in North Vietnam on 23 December, 1972. He was a pilot on board a F-4 Phantom, which crashed after apparently being struck by hostile fire. His parachute was sighted going down in enemy territory. Other details are unknown at this time. However, they will be furnished to you as soon as they are known. Pending further information, he will be listed officially as missing in action. If you have any questions, contact our Casualty Assistance Officer. Please accept my sincere sympathy during this period of anxiety.*

*Sincerely,*
*Major General Timothy Arnold, Commander*
*Air Force Military Personnel Center*
*Randolph AFB, TX*

Wynne held the report to her chest, tears streaming down her face. Jean placed her arms around her friend and the two sobbed uncontrollably.

"Wynne, could I call your mother and Michael's mother for you?" Jean asked quietly, dabbing at her eyes.

"Of course, that has to be done," Wynne said, wishing she could spare her mother and mother-in-law the agony she was feeling. "Their numbers are by the telephone."

"Should we awaken the children, too, and let them know?" Jean asked.

"No, let's wait until later," Wynne said.

Jean hugged Wynne and slipped into the kitchen, returning a few minutes later to her anxious friend. "Your mother said, she'd come if you want her to. She's waiting to hear from you."

"She doesn't need to come," Wynne said. "Michael will be found soon. They'll be calling to let me know before long." Her voice broke, betraying the doubt she was trying to deny.

Jean put her arm around Wynne's shoulder.

"Won't he have a great war story to tell us when he gets home?" she asked. Her lighthearted laughter sounded more like crying, and finally they both wept quietly together. Jean dabbed her eyes with a tissue. "I'll take Jon and Emily to school, and be right back."

The house was very quiet after Jean left until Stephen and Lauren awakened.

"Mom, what's wrong?" Lauren asked as she saw her mother's tear-stained face.

Wynne sat Stephen and Lauren on the sofa beside her. "I need to tell you about Daddy," Wynne said, her voice tensing. "He had to bail out of his airplane, but I'm sure he's fine."

"He's still coming home isn't he?" Lauren asked, her chin quivering.

"Sure he is!" Stephen said, his own eyes clouding with tears.

"Of course, Darling," Wynne said embracing both children and holding back tears. "We'll just have to wait a little longer."

Wynne somehow managed to get through the day listening expectantly for the telephone to ring with news from the Commander's office. But the telephone was ominously silent except for several calls from her mother.

***

### January, 1973

THE EARLY WEEKS of January were a blur for Wynne as the days passed without any further word on Michel's fate. As the peace talks proceeded, even Michael's beloved Miami Dolphins won the Super Bowl on January 14th. She imagined his loud whoop when he read the clipping she'd mailed, *Miami Dolphins 14, Washington Redskins, 7.*

On Saturday, January 20th, Wynne watched the TV news as President Richard Nixon and Vice-President Spiro Agnew were sworn in for their second terms of office. It gave her even more of a sense of assurance Michael would be home soon as she watched the glittering inaugural activities at the nation's Capitol.

During a fitful sleep, she dreamed of seeing Michael ejecting from a burning plane. His parachute seemed to disappear into a dark forest. She cried out to him, but received no response. She awakened, lay awake for hours, and found herself staring at the snapshot of Michael she kept on her bedside table. It had been taken the first year they were married --the eager young officer with his new lieutenant's bars looked back at her with the confident smile she had thought would always be there for her. She held on to the picture momentarily before replacing it in its accustomed place, and turning off the bedside lamp.

***

WYNNE WAS LINGERING over a second cup of coffee the next morning after she had taken Stephen and Lauren to school when she heard a knock on the kitchen door. She saw Jean's husband, Ray, through the curtains and opened the door. Ray was also part of Michael's 58th Tactical Fighter Squadron from Eglin. The majority of their group had been deployed to the Thai Royal Air Force Base in Ubon, Thailand.

He fingered his hat nervously, yet his erect military bearing reminded her so much of Michael.

"Ray...do come in, and join me for a cup of coffee."

"Wynne, I felt you would like to hear about the rescue attempts."

"Attempts? Then they've..." Wynne's said as her spirits lifted.

"No," he quickly added. "They haven't found Michael. I just thought if you knew how it was done you'd feel better."

Wynne nodded and sat back down at the kitchen table as Ray sat across from her, his face etched with concern.

"There's a coordinator for the rescue team," Ray explained. "They have airborne and ground radios and radar. With this information they can direct the fighters and choppers to the correct position of the downed crewman."

"How do they keep the enemy from getting there first?" Wynne asked, her body tensing as she could see Michael fleeing for his life in the jungle.

"We have the 3rd Aerospace Rescue and Recovery Group. They coordinate all search and rescue efforts. They send a pair of A-1 Skyraiders known as Sandies to contact the downed airman by radio. Another rescue helicopter goes in -- probably a HH-3 Jolly Green Giant. Other aircraft fly protective cover for the rescuers."

"Can they really protect and rescue him?" Wynne asked.

"They do an incredible job, Wynne. If there's a chance that he's still alive --even though it's in enemy territory, they'll do their best. Those guys don't give up." He hesitated for a moment and then added, "Of course, Wynne, you have to be prepared for the fact that sometimes the enemy uses the airman's emergency survival homing device to lure SAR helicopters into a trap. So the fact there may have been a radio transmission doesn't prove that Michael is alive."

Icy fear seized her heart.

"That's all I want to say," Ray said. "Just wanted you to know our boys are out there for him."

"I know that..." Wynne whispered as Ray stood to leave. "They will find him...I have to believe that."

\*\*\*

LATER ONE EVENING as she read a newspaper account of President Lyndon Johnson's funeral, she couldn't help but notice the coincidence of the date of his death at the LBJ Ranch on January 22nd. It was one month after Michael's plane was shot down. This war that had divided a nation had essentially cost Lyndon Johnson the presidency, as its burden had made him choose not to seek re-election in 1968.

*And what was this war going to cost her? Not Michael, dear God. Please not Michael!*

# Chapter Two

*January, 1973*

WYNNE WENT TO the Gallery the next morning. *Perhaps working would keep her mind occupied until they found Michael. He just had to be found safe.* She would allow herself to think of no other possibility. *Safe.*

Sunlight streamed into the darkened room when she opened the large wooden door of the Gallery. The warm cedar interior dispelled some of the chill she felt. She entered and saw fiber art of all kinds – bright colors catching sunlight reflected off the Gulf through wide picture windows on the south, the darker, mood pieces lighted subtly on the western wall. As Wynne went to her office, she heard the front door of the Gallery open.

"It's only me," called Connie, her co-worker.

Wynne felt a sense of relief at not being alone – especially not now. The bubbly chatter from Connie would be a welcome diversion. Connie Evans had served as the Gallery's Girl Friday – hostess, secretary, accountant, and maintenance person – it all seemed to fall into her job description. Her work let Wynne concentrate on the creative aspects of the Gallery, and to pursue her own fiber art.

Connie stuck her head in the office. "Hi! How are you?" Her brow furrowed. "Any more word on Michael?" Her cheerful tone lifted Wynne's hopes.

Wynne shook her head.

"You'll hear soon," Connie assured, walking briskly to the desk and giving Wynne a hug. "What's on the agenda for you today?" she asked.

"Getting the new pottery display ready," Wynne replied. "Anna's work needs maximum exposure before she leaves."

Connie nodded as she turned to leave. "Let me know if I can help...I'm almost through with the purchasing orders and correspondence. Lorraine's here, too. I'm sure she'd be glad to help."

"I will," Wynne said, following Connie out of the office. Wynne stopped to chat briefly with

Lorraine Marshall, the Gallery's watercolor artist, as she worked on a seascape.

"That's a lovely scene, Lorraine. You've captured the gracefulness of the sea oats perfectly," Wynne noted.

"They do have a special character," Lorraine said, adding an extra brushstroke to some of the tall grasses. Her face grew somber. "Everything will be okay," Lorraine assured and gently squeezed Wynne's hand.

Wynne nodded and tried to smile, but it seemed as though she had forgotten how. Lorraine's lips trembled and she looked away. "Oh, Wynne," she sobbed. "I'm such a cry baby..."

"It's O.K., Lorraine. He'll be O.K.," Wynne said, unexpectedly the comforter.

The hours passed quickly as Wynne prepared the pottery display. Her potter friend, Anna McRae, was a master at her craft. The glazes and designs were of museum quality. Wynne felt certain the pieces would be well-received by Gallery patrons. She worked until lunchtime carefully placing various pieces of pottery amid fiber pieces for their best display. She would miss Anna who soon would be leaving with her husband for a new assignment in England.

Keeping busy had helped Wynne to get through the morning. She would plan to stay as busy as possible, perhaps not allowing time for anything but the Gallery. *Could she focus solely on that?* She would try, at least. A routine would surely sustain her and provide armor against the unexpected – and everything was unexpected.

As the afternoon progressed, Wynne found her first feeling of peace in the Gallery work. It felt good to have a sense of purpose again after the numbness of last evening. *How have other military wives coped?* She carefully placed a ceramic bowl on a fiber placemat. "He will be found soon," she said aloud firmly, as though the statement could will it to happen.

*\*\*\**

DURING JANUARY WYNNE focused on the Gallery. One day Jean burst into the room where Wynne was working.

Wynne glanced up from her display in surprise. "Jean, why are you..."

Her friend quickly embraced her and blurted out, "Wynne, have you heard the news? The

Vietnam Peace Agreement was signed today in Paris. The war is over!"

Jean's radiant face expressed the feelings welling up in Wynne – *the war was over! Now the ground forces could search for Michael. If he were wounded, or being hidden by friendly Vietnamese – or even a P.O.W., he could return home safely.* She hugged Jean and they whirled around in an awkward little dance, their faces radiant and tearful.

At home that evening after Stephen and Lauren were asleep, Wynne eagerly read the newspaper account of the peace agreement. The date – January 27th – would be a date she would always remember. Yet a feeling of despair swept over her. Her chest tightened with anger as she looked at the photograph of the representatives of North and South Vietnam, the United States, and the Viet Cong as they formally signed the Peace Accords in Paris. She covered the photograph with her hand, and crumpled it in her fist.

\*\*\*

AS SHE UNLOCKED her front door the following Tuesday afternoon, an official blue Air Force staff car pulled into the driveway. Colonel Rutledge and Jean Stearns emerged. *They must have found Michael!* Wynne hurried across the driveway to meet them. But she stopped when she saw the stricken expression on her friend's face. A cold fear washed over her. "No!" she cried.

"Wynne, we do have more word," Colonel Rutledge said softly, "Shall we go inside?"

Jean took Wynne by the arm, and they walked silently into her living room. Wynne felt herself being drawn into hopelessness.

"Debriefings of Michael's last flight have revealed that his wingman, Tom Markham, spotted Michael and his parachute. It was snarled in a tree..." Colonel Rutledge said.

"Then he's all right," Wynne said, but the air in the room seemed heavy with an oppressive sadness. The faces looking back at her were joyless.

Colonel Rutledge took a long breath. "I'm afraid not. A helicopter team surveyed the crash site wreckage where his plane had gone down. Additional flights over a period of days took photographs of your husband in his 'chute. They've been studied by medical experts, who agree that from the attitude of his body and no indication of movement, he was apparently dead."

*Apparently dead. How could anyone be apparently dead?*

Wynne listened in disbelief. *Not Michael. Not her Michael. No, God. He was not dead. They had said "apparently". They weren't sure. No...he couldn't be dead.*

*I won't cry in front of Colonel Rutledge.* She fought the tears welling in her eyes. *Michael wouldn't want me to cry. He'll be so proud of me when he gets back.*

Jean stood and put her arm around her friend. "I'm so sorry, Wynne. So sorry..."

*Why did Jean keep saying that? Why didn't she say, "It isn't true! It isn't true!"*

Jean's tears spilled on Wynne's shoulder. *Jean shouldn't cry. He isn't dead. There are a thousand other explanations,* Wynne reasoned. *Friendly Vietnamese peasants have found him. They are probably hiding him, and he's just waiting for rescue. Or maybe it wasn't his parachute...Of course, it wasn't Michael's parachute. Didn't they all look alike from the air?*

Colonel Rutledge continued. "It's uncertain the North Vietnamese will let U.S. reconnaissance teams remain in country to retrieve bodies...I'm very sorry." He paused before continuing. "Michael's efforts during the bombing mission were

28

heroic, Mrs. Reardon. His commander has recommended him for a Congressional Medal of Honor." He added, "This is the nation's highest military award for valor."

Wynne caught her breath. *The military's highest honor! Body...why does he speak of Michael's body? Michael isn't dead. As long as she believed that, he would be found safe and sound. And a Congressional Medal of Honor award would surely please him and validate all he believed in. She could see him standing proudly at attention accepting the award.*

Colonel Rutledge handed her the official letter from the Casualty Office. As disbelief overwhelmed her, she read the message.

*Dear Mrs. Reardon:*

*It is with deep personal sympathy that I officially inform you your husband is no longer considered missing in action in North Vietnam. His body was sighted near the North Vietnam border on 23 December, and he is now officially listed as killed in action, body not recovered. He was on a strike mission of the highest priority.*

*Maj. Reardon was piloting one of a flight of F-4 aircraft engaged in a fire suppression mission, Operation Linebacker, designed to destroy a key antiaircraft defensive complex. This complex contained surface-to-air missiles (SAM), an exceptionally heavy concentration of antiaircraft artillery, and other automatic weapons. The defensive network was situated to dominate the approach and provide protection to an important North Vietnam industrial center. Fighter bombers were scheduled to attack immediately after the strike by Maj. Reardon's flight.*

*In the initial attack on the defensive complex the lead aircraft was crippled, and Maj. Reardon's aircraft was extensively damaged by the intense enemy fire. Maj. Reardon radioed his wingman that his Weapon Systems Officer, 1st Lt. Jeremy Marshall, had been killed. Reardon realized that the success of the impending fighter bomber attack on the center now depended on his ability to effectively suppress the defensive fire. He took over the weapons controls from 1st Lt. Marshall. Maj. Reardon ignored the enemy's overwhelming firepower and the damage to his aircraft, and pressed his attack. Despite a continuing hail of antiaircraft fire, deadly surface-to-air missiles, and counterattacks by MIG interceptors, Maj. Reardon flew repeated close range strikes to silence the enemy defensive positions with bombs and air-to-ground missiles.*

*His action in rendering ineffective the defensive SAM and antiaircraft artillery sites enabled the ensuing fighter bombers to strike successfully the important industrial target without loss or damage to their aircraft. These actions appreciably reduced the enemy's ability to provide essential war materiel. He also went to the aid of a wingman whose plane was in trouble. After his successful bombing mission of a strategic target, his plane received extensive enemy fire. He was seen ejecting about dusk from his disabled plane. The extensive enemy fire destroyed his aircraft, resulting in his tragic sacrifice.*

*Maj. Reardon's consummate skill, extraordinary heroism, and intrepidity at the cost of his life, above and beyond the call of duty, are in the highest traditions of military service. His valor reflects great credit upon himself, his unit, and the U.S. Air Force.*

*This war brought forth the highest nobility in our fighting men and Major Reardon met this challenge. Because of his heroism, he has been recommended to receive posthumously our nation's highest medal of valor -- the Congressional Medal of Honor. It is brave men like Major Reardon who make America the strong nation that it is. I share in your time of sorrow.*

*Sincerely,*

*Major General Timothy Arnold*
*Commander Air Force Military Personnel Center*
*Randolph AFB, TX*

"Please call me if there's anything that I can do for you or the children," Colonel Rutledge said. He put his hand on Wynne's shoulder as he turned to leave. "Major Reardon was a brave pilot."

Wynne only nodded as Jean followed him to the door. She caught her breath. *How could Michael be shot down on December 23rd? That was only six days before President Nixon had ordered a halt to the bombing in Vietnam on December 29th! Six days...*

"I'll get the children from school," Jean said. "I'll be right back."

***

WYNNE CLUNG TO the hope Michael was still alive for several weeks. Her friends and other military personnel paid visits of condolence. They remarked how strong she was. Jean seemed anxious about her, and brought meals for her and the children each day. Wynne questioned why Michael had to go to Tom's aid. She would ask Colonel Rutledge the next time she talked with him.

Stephen and Lauren seemed bewildered by their mother's sadness, and all of the attention of their parents' friends in the military community.

"Daddy's strong and tough. He'll make it, Mom," Stephen would say when he would find her crying in an unguarded moment.

"Daddy will come home," Lauren would assure her often, too.

*Their lack of understanding of the gravity of Michael's peril in enemy territory was a blessing.* Wynne continued to listen for the telephone and official word that would reverse the presumed dead report, but only her mother's well-meaning calls from New Orleans persisted.

"I can be there in a few hours," Elizabeth Carmichael assured.

"No, Mother. I'm fine. Really!"

Of course, she wasn't fine. But she couldn't stand her mother's suffocating concern. As well-meaning as her mother was, Wynne felt it would still be easier for her to handle things herself so the "I'm fine" response never wavered.

***

SHE CALLED THE Pentagon for more word on what was being done to find him. Why weren't they searching the villages along the North Vietnam border?

She refused to accept their explanation that, even if he had survived the parachute landing, there was no way to disguise an American of his stature as a Vietnamese peasant. But Michael had taken survival training. She remembered that vigorous time at the Stead Air Force Base Survival School in Nevada. He'd made it through as a 'survivor' in their mock war. The training there in the Sierra Nevada mountains  taught him how to survive if forced down in remote or unfriendly terrain, how to escape capture, and how to escape if captured.  He could survive if anyone could. *Perhaps he was in a cave living off the land...perhaps.*

\*\*\*

AN ADMINISTRATIVE ASSISTANT took her calls to William Rogers' State Department office graciously.  The office assured her that the word she had received from the Casualty Office was correct. Major Reardon was no longer listed as an MIA.  He was presumed dead.  When would she like to have the Memorial Service?  It could be held at Eglin Air Force Base near where she lived.  And his squadron would participate in the ceremony -- would fly the missing man formation.

She refused to accept the finality of a Memorial Service.  There would have to be a body; some proof that Michael had not survived. Sometimes, in weaker moments, she wondered if she might be asking too much of him -- was she prolonging his suffering with her hope.  *Would it be kinder to accept his death now than to keep him alive --*

*fleeing, hiding, hungry, or captured, only to die later, never to come home?* But she could not let go.

The gentle urging of her mother, friends, and the base Chaplain were to no avail. She was single-minded in her belief that Michael had survived and would return. She clung to hope, a hope buoyed by a letter that she received from him two weeks after he was reported shot down. It was postmarked the day of his last flight. She refused to open the letter. As long as it was unopened, she somehow felt he would remain alive. She placed the letter in front of his picture, promising herself they would open it -- read it together when he came home.

***

THE DAYS PASSED into weeks. Chaplain Turner called frequently, and even recommended that she talk to the base psychiatrist. "Wynne, he's helped other families through similar situations. Please see him."

Calls from the Casualty Office became less frequent, although they were always cordial to her when she called.

"No further word, Mrs. Reardon. We're sorry..." the Casualty Officer said.

She read in the newspaper where National Security Advisor and Secretary of State, Henry Kissinger, had gone to Hanoi to discuss the cease-fire and handle aid arrangements. If she'd only known in advance about his trip, she could have sought his aid to help find Michael. She was angry at the thought of the lost opportunity.

\*\*\*

RAY STOPPED BY to explain in more detail the circumstances of Michael's forced bailout. "He tried to get away from the artillery, Wynne. He rolled, climbed, and dove until the Phantom's hydraulic system took a hit and the fluid drained out. Then there was no way to control the bird ..."

Ray held Wynne's hand as he continued. "Tom saw the fluid spewing out of the plane, and Michael's unsuccessful attempts to control it. Michael had to bail out, but he had a good 'chute. It came down in a heavily wooded area. There was a strong signal coming from the beeper on his radio. That's how Tom spotted him, but there was never any communication from Michael despite numerous attempts to contact him on the radio."

"Did he see it coming?" Wynne asked.

"I'm sure that he saw the green glow on the screen when their radar locked on to him. The system buzzer is unmistakable," he said in a soft voice, remembering those missions where he had to jink out of the way of enemy fire. The image of that haunting green glow had stayed with him. He knew that was probably the last thing Michael saw before he hit the ejection button. Ray avoided mention of the danger of the ejection itself, but Wynne probably already knew that.

Even Ray's frank appraisal of Michael's last mission did not convince Wynne that her husband probably did not survive. Her optimism was still determinedly in place.

\*\*\*

February, 1973

THE EARLY FEBRUARY news brought word that the U.S. Senate had established a Select Committee on Presidential Campaign Activities to investigate the events surrounding break-in at the Democratic

National Committee Headquarters in the Watergate building complex in Washington, D.C. the previous June. As Wynne glanced at the article, she wondered what could possibly interest a burglar at a political party's office -- and in light of the monumental news that the Vietnam War had ended, why such a minor break-in deserved national news attention the previous June and again now. It seemed to overshadow the news Wynne listened for intently.

***

THE FIRST POWS were released on February 12th. Although the Casualty Office had already provided Wynne a list of names, she eagerly scanned the faces on the TV screen as the men disembarked at Clark Air Force Base in the Philippines. POW status reports on others still held in captivity were provided in late February and early March. Major Michael Reardon's name was never on any of the lists.

Her feelings of despair were reflected in the cold wind that brought remnants of winter out of the north. She had never experienced the sense of bleakness she now felt. Although she was rarely alone, she was lonely, so lonely.

***

## March - April, 1973

WYNNE HELD TO the hope that perhaps his name had simply been overlooked. From February 12th to April 4th, "Operation Homecoming" scheduled 54 C-141 missions to fly 591 American POWs captured in Southeast Asia from Hanoi to Clark Air Base in the Philippines, and then on to Travis Air Force Base, CA. She watched on the evening news on April 4th as the jubilant families embraced their returning loved ones. Michael Reardon remained MIA in her heart and mind. She would get names and addresses of these returning POWs -- write to them. *Maybe they knew where Michael was.*

In subsequent newscasts, the returning POWs began relating accounts of physical and mental torture inflicted on them during their captivity. "Oh, God, please don't let Michael suffer wherever he is," she prayed, wishing desperately that he were alive, yet fearing for his well-being if he were.

Wynne continued to attend Sunday morning services at the base Chapel where she and Michael had often worshipped. Reassurance swept over her when the congregation sang the familiar songs of faith. The words of the Air Force hymn, "Lord, Guard and Guide the Men Who Fly", comforted her as the refrain "...uphold them with Thy saving grace..." echoed throughout the sanctuary one Sunday in early April. Bright rays of spring sunshine streamed through the stained glass windows as though in affirmation.

## Chapter Three

### May, 1973

WYNNE PLUNGED INTO work at the Gallery to keep from thinking about her lonely future or anything else. On her desk she found a number of letters of condolence from friends who had just learned about Michael's death, and two resumes to fill the position of potter at the Gallery. One was from a man named Jason Garrison. His credentials seemed impressive -- a Masters of Fine Arts from the University of California at Berkeley, and extensive experience in galleries. The second resume was from a woman, a recent graduate from an Art Institute with no gallery experience. She marked her calendar to give Jason Garrison a call for an interview.

Among the letters she opened was an invitation to the Cedar Key Art show that would begin on Memorial Day – Monday, May 28th.

Approximately 150 of the state's best artisans would assemble for three days to display wares, compare talents, and evaluate the quality of their work.

Memories of previous trips there flooded back as Wynne remembered the fun she and Michael always had at the event, and the many friends they had made through the years. She could almost smell the aroma of frying mullet that the Volunteer Fire Department always prepared in abundance, and see the rows of makeshift tents that spilled down the sandy shore to the water's edge. Maybe attending the event would give her some purpose in life again -- it was something to look forward to and plan for -- a goal she desperately needed. It was a premiere gathering of Florida artists and would be good exposure for the Gallery. She needed to work to make Shoreline Gallery as successful as possible, and attending this particular invitational event would be a good start.

She remembered the Cedar Key show two years ago when Michael went with her. It had been like a second honeymoon prior to his leaving for Vietnam. She remembered the weekend of love they had shared, every nuance, every endearment.

Brushing the memories aside, she turned her attention to designing a fiber piece for the Cedar

Key event. Her concentration was broken again and again by unanswered questions about Tom's actions prior to Michael's death. Despite efforts to dismiss this concern from her mind, she kept seeing Michael's parachute hanging in a tree.

Wynne gave her attention back to the fiber piece on the worktable. The nature tapestry began to take shape as she wove driftwood, palm spathes, and tree bark into the warp. She held the piece out at arm's length for inspection and thought with a sigh, *if only life could be as easy as the rhythm of weaving.*

The ringing of the telephone interrupted her thoughts. She reached across the worktable to answer it.

"Shoreline Gallery."

"Wynne Reardon?" a male voice asked.

"Yes..."

"This is Jason Garrison. I believe we have a 3:00 o'clock appointment today."

Wynne caught her breath. Of course, she'd written the interview with the potter on her office calendar earlier, but had failed to check her schedule.

"Yes, we do. Please come on over."

"Fine, I'll be there shortly."

She liked his voice -- warm and resonant.

*At last. Perhaps we can have a full-time potter to meet the demand.* Anna McRae had only worked part time because of the demands of her family, and her pieces sold as quickly as they were completed. A good supply of quality pottery would help ensure the Gallery's success.

***

WYNNE LOOKED ACROSS her desk at Jason Garrison, tall and at ease in well-worn jeans and a knit shirt. Despite his casual clothing, he appeared more like a college professor than an artist. His short-cropped black hair, graying at the temples, gave him a look of distinction, and his brown eyes added an intensity she hoped would be reflected in his work.

"Wynne Reardon," she said extending her hand across the desk. "Your experience is most impressive...your Gallery work especially."

Jason clasped her hand and had a bemused look as she spoke, almost as though he were humoring a child. Wynne noted gentleness in his handshake that seemed to belie the power she sensed was there.

"I believe I can produce what Shoreline Gallery needs," he said. "When do I start?"

Wynne laughed. "Well, this is only my first interview…I need time to consider the other applicants."

Jason stood as though he were almost standing at attention, and said brusquely, "Well, you need a potter. Obviously you're familiar with my work. Why would you consider other applicants? You need me. I'm here."

Wynne looked at his resume again, trying to keep from smiling at this upstart. After a brief hesitation she said, "You're right -- how about tomorrow?"

"Fine -- I'll unload my equipment," he said. "The base salary I indicated on my resume is firm. Reasonable and firm. My commissioned pieces are a firm ninety percent. That is not negotiable. When I put your Gallery on the map, then you can afford what I'm worth." He turned to leave and then paused. "By the way, you don't have enough display area for the pottery. I'll build some shelves, even though it's not in my job description."

She wondered, *What have I done?* as Jason strode out of her office. "I'll build some shelves," she mimicked. *Indeed!* And Anna had received only seventy-five percent on her commissioned sales, but then she didn't have Jason's credentials, or reputation as a potter despite her excellent work. Wynne was almost angry with herself for being intimidated into hiring him on the spot, but his credentials were impeccable. There was also something intriguing about his personality she couldn't resist. He was so unlike Michael in appearance and demeanor, yet there was something in his spirit...She chided herself for even drawing the comparison.

***

WYNNE TOOK STEPHEN and Lauren to the Gallery with her on Monday since it was a school holiday. They found Jason waiting in her office. He was holding Michael's photograph in his hand, and put it down on the desk when they entered.

"I didn't realize there was a Major Reardon," he said.

Wynne steadied her voice. "Yes...he was presumed to be killed in Vietnam."

Jason remained expressionless at her reply. His only comment was, "I see."

Wynne considered this non-committal response strange, and gave him a sharp look.

"I need to order some supplies," Jason said unruffled, handing her a list. "The supplier's address is attached."

Wynne nodded. "Fine...I'll order them." She turned to Stephen and Lauren. "Jason, this is my son Stephen and my daughter Lauren. Children this is Jason Garrison...he's our new potter."

Jason extended his hand to Stephen. "Nice to meet you, Stephen. And you, Lauren," he said tousling her hair.

"Yes, Sir," Stephen said.

Lauren just looked shyly at him and asked, "Will you teach me how to make pottery?"

"Of course, Jason...at your service," he said with a low bow.

"Now children, go play in the workroom," their mother suggested.

As Stephen and Lauren left the office, Jason watched them.

"Nice kids," he said with a smile.

"I think so," Wynne replied.

Jason straightened the photograph before leaving the room, but it was not in its accustomed place. Wynne moved it to the opposite side of her desk as an act of defiance. "Insensitive," she muttered at Jason's thoughtlessness in putting the photograph back on her desk in the wrong place.

\*\*\*

WHEN WYNNE ARRIVED home for lunch on Tuesday, she found an envelope from Colonel Rutledge's office in her mailbox. "Probably another form to fill out," she murmured as she tore open the envelope. Instead of a form, it was a personal letter.

> *Dear Mrs. Reardon:*
>
> *We are having a special Memorial Day ceremony on Monday, May 28th, at Eglin Air Force Base at 1400 hours. Base personnel who have received awards this past year will be honored at this time. Would you please come as our special guest and represent your late husband in this day of recognition?*

*Sincerely,*
*Colonel Craig Rutledge*
*Squadron Group Commander, Eglin AFB.*

Wynne went to her desk and flipped the pages of her calendar to Memorial Day. Cedar Key Art Show was written boldly across the date of Monday, May 28th.

*Jason will have to attend and represent the Gallery,* she decided. She couldn't possibly miss a ceremony where there would be a tribute for Michael, even though it would mean missing the trip to Cedar Key, a trip she had counted on and looked forward to with such anticipation. Since Stephen and Lauren were spending that weekend with Mrs. Reardon, Wynne had thought that her trip to the Art Show would be assured.

\*\*\*

WHEN SHE RETURNED to the Gallery, she took a copy of the Cedar Key Art Show brochure to Jason's work area. He was busy working on new display shelves.

"I have a conflict on Memorial Day," Wynne said, putting the schedule down on the worktable.

Jason continued to hammer furiously.

Wynne tapped him on the shoulder and shouted, "Would you take our exhibit to the Cedar Key Art show on Memorial Day?"

He responded to her request with a level gaze. His eyes seemed to look through her. "Sure, but you'll be missing one of the best art shows in the state."

Wynne flinched. She didn't have to be reminded this was the premiere gathering of Florida artists.

"I know...it can't be helped," she said curtly. "I'll have several fiber pieces and Lorraine will have a number of paintings. Please include any work you'd like to take, too." Her strident voice seemed to be coming from someone else.

Jason looked at her with a quizzical expression as she turned and hurried to her office.

*Wynne, you have to get a grip on yourself.* She closed the door. *There will be other Art Shows.*

She looked at Michael's smiling picture on her desk, and felt guilty for having any regrets about attending the Memorial Day ceremony at Eglin.

\*\*\*

*Monday, May 28, 1973*

WYNNE SHIELDED HER eyes from the sun as the F-4 jets streaked across the brilliant blue sky at the Memorial Day Ceremony. A sigh caught in her throat as she watched the missing man formation honoring those who had given their lives for their country. Other dignitaries and award recipients watched the flawless performance until the planes disappeared from view.

Colonel Rutledge read a list of awards. Each person stood and was acknowledged with generous applause by the audience.

"...and we are honored to have Major Michael Reardon's wife with us today. She will soon receive his Congressional Medal of Honor, posthumously."

Wynne stood and bowed ever so slightly to acknowledge applause from the audience.

After the ceremony, many who had known Michael greeted her. She never ceased to be amazed by the extent of his contacts. His pilot network was worldwide. John Ratliff, his wingman while they were stationed at Hickam, gave her a warm embrace. And Frank Ronsom, a colleague from flight school, offered his condolences.

She left the platform and walked by the Honor Guard, which stood stiffly at attention. Jean and Ray met her on the grassy hill where families still lingered. Children ran playing amid the pine trees while their parents visited.

"That was a lovely ceremony," Jean said, putting her arm around Wynne.

Wynne nodded as she watched the American flag fluttering in the breeze. It seemed only yesterday she and Michael had watched the Thunderbirds perform. In fact, it had been two years ago on the Fourth of July. *Would time ever pass so quickly again?* It seemed unlikely.

\*\*\*

THE NEXT DAY Wynne worked on her nature tapestry. The Gallery seemed unusually quiet without the hum of the potter's wheel.

*How were things progressing at the Art Show?* She still felt a twinge of remorse at being unable to attend. It was the first official invitation for Shoreline Gallery, such a compliment to be included with the state's outstanding artists.

Her thoughts were interrupted by Jean's voice.

"Lunch time!" Jean called out, struggling into the Gallery with a giant picnic hamper.

Wynne smiled and put down her tapestry. "What a nice surprise..."

"I bet you could use a break," Jean said as she brought out fruit, cheese, and sandwiches from the depths of the basket.

"Sorry you had to miss the Art Show," she said as she arranged the food on the worktable. "I know your heart was set on it."

"There will be others," Wynne replied. 'I'm sure Jason is representing Shoreline Gallery well."

"He's a strange fellow," Jean said. "I tried to talk about Berkeley. Ray took some courses there, but Jason changed the subject. What do you really know about him?"

Wynne looked surprised at Jean's question.

"He has excellent credentials -- a MFA from Berkeley and experience in some of the finest galleries...and he's a Grade A handyman. That's almost too much to expect."

"Strange he would choose an obscure little Gallery in Florida," Jean remarked.

"I think he's probably a serial killer hiding out here," Wynne said, and they both laughed -- something she had done too little of lately. "Location maybe?" Wynne asked more seriously.

"Well, I imagine you'll get an interesting story from him someday," Jean said, still smiling.

\*\*\*

WYNNE RECEIVED A telephone call from her mother just as she unlocked her front door.

"Wynne...I was afraid that you had already left for Cedar Key," Elizabeth Carmichael said.

"Hello, Mother...I didn't go to Cedar Key. Colonel Rutledge invited me to a ceremony at the base. I just couldn't say no."

Her mother sighed. "Now, Wynne...you must get on with your life. And your life now is your Gallery."

Wynne blanched at her mother's frankness, although she wasn't surprised.

"But, mother...I couldn't miss a ceremony that honors Michael. I just couldn't."

"The Cedar Key Art Show would provide many important contacts, Wynne. Keep that in mind."

Wynne learned long ago it was futile to argue with her mother and replied, "I know, Mother. Our new potter Jason Garrison is representing Shoreline Gallery."

"Well, Dear, please don't miss any more art opportunities yourself. How are you feeling? Not losing any more weight I hope..." She went on at length with advice on nutrition and exercise, and more suggestions concerning the Gallery.

After hanging up the telephone, Wynne reflected on her mother's reminder: "Your life now is your Gallery." *But her life, too, was as the widow of Major Michael Reardon. She couldn't escape that responsibility -- not now and perhaps not ever.*

\*\*\*

WYNNE WAS SURPRISED to hear the hum of the potter's wheel when she opened the Gallery early on Tuesday morning. She found Jason already at work, and noticed the shelves were finished. She observed they were of craftsman quality, and realized she was indeed fortunate to have someone so versatile and capable at the Gallery.

"My, you must have received some good commissions for your pieces," Wynne said, watching his industrious activity. The revolving action of the spinning wheel mesmerized her for a moment as she watched the clay vessel slowly taking shape. Droplets of water flew from the wet clay as it twirled on the wheel. Jason's strong hands caressed the clay, and molded it gently into shape.

"As a matter of fact, I did," he said, not bothering to look up from the wheel. "You didn't do so badly either."

"Me?" Wynne asked.

"Yes, the Emerald Towers in Miami wants another mandala to match the one they bought earlier. Their order's on your desk. The interior decorator gave me a card -- it's somewhere on or in my desk if you need it. Just imagine the other contacts you'd had if you'd been there yourself." He looked up at her with a smile.

"You sound like my mother," she scolded.

Wynne tried to ignore his last remark since she didn't need another reminder about the value of personal contacts. *How could Jason, or even her mother for that matter, possibly understand her responsibilities to her husband?*

"You're a fine artist," he said. "It was a pleasure representing your work."

His eyes held her for a long time. She felt a strange sense of attraction toward him that she couldn't deny. The look in those brown eyes aroused feelings she found hard to dismiss.

"I thought you might like a cup of coffee," Wynne said handing him a steaming mug.

He sipped the hot coffee carefully. "How do you manage always to make such a perfect cup?" he asked, meeting her gaze.

"Practice makes perfect," I guess she said with a laugh, glancing away from him. "And what is this *objet d'art* going to be?" she asked, looking at the clay on the wheel.

Jason laughed. "Good grief! Surely you don't have to ask. Have I completely lost my touch? This award winning piece will be a flower vase for the center of an elegant table."

Wynne smiled and tried to avoid his look as she said, "Thanks for the order. How was the Art Show overall?"

"Well attended and quite professional...many people asked about you. Your fiber pieces are in great demand."

"That's good to hear...I'd better get to work on some. The shelves are perfect," she said, rubbing her hand over the smooth wood.

Jason nodded -- his hands never missing a turn on the wheel as a perfect bowl emerged.

As she went to her workbench, she felt his eyes following her, but she didn't dare look back.

Wynne thought about the order from the Emerald Towers. It was truly a realization of her dream to have a piece of such magnitude bought and another ordered.

*Who was the hotel buyer? She'd like to call him or her and thank them for the order.* She went to Jason's work area to ask him for the card he'd mentioned, but the potter's wheel was silent, and he was nowhere to be found. She stopped at his workbench where neat rows of his recent pieces of pottery were stored. She marveled at their beauty and perfection.

While she rubbed the smooth surface of a perfectly designed bowl with her hand, she noticed his cluttered desk. Several soft drink cans, numerous art catalogs, and an assortment of glazes were strewn about. *Another characteristic so unlike Michael.* She remembered his very ordered life.

*Where did he put the card?* She glanced at the clutter. Looking through the center drawer, she found only a collection of carving tools, pens, and pencils.

She pulled out the right top drawer of the desk. The hotel interior decorator's card lay amid a number of newspaper clippings. Curious, she opened one of the folded pieces of paper. A different looking Jason was pictured receiving a trophy at a hang gliding competition. She hardly recognized him -- his hair was shoulder length and he had a beard. Only the eyes and smile were familiar. The caption dated July 17, 1969 read -- LOCAL POTTER WINS DISTANCE EVENT IN HANG GLIDER COMPETITION.

As Wynne unfolded the second clipping, a smaller article fell out. *Another contest?* She read the article captioned August 22, 1972, Miami Beach, FL,

GROUP OF VIETNAM WAR PROTESTERS INTERRUPT REPUBLICAN NATIONAL CONVENTION. A similar picture of Jason greeted her although this time he didn't hold a trophy. Instead it was a sign that read U.S. OUT OF VIETNAM.

Her heart sank. *How could Jason have been a Vietnam War protester?* She felt a sense of complete betrayal. *So that's how he spent his time at Berkeley -- hiding behind protest signs while Michael defended his country!* Anger raged within her. She crumpled the clipping, and dropped it back into the drawer.

***

WHEN JASON RETURNED to the Gallery, Wynne was sitting at his desk.

He smiled when he saw her. "To what do I owe this visit?" he asked. "I assume we covered the Art Show completely."

"How could you do it?" she asked defiantly.

"Do it?" Jason looked puzzled. "I'm sorry, Wynne. I'll have to plead not guilty until I know what the charges are." He grinned like a schoolboy.

61

"This is no joking matter, Jason," Wynne said, pulling the crumpled article out of his desk drawer.

"Oh," said Jason as she pressed open the clipping, and laid it on the desk.

His face darkened and deep lines scored his forehead.

"We should never have been involved there. It was a no win situation. Too bad it took ten years, three million servicemen in-country, and 58,000 American bodies to learn that." He paused, and looking very pensive, added, "The Vietnam War was filled with tactical victories. We won most of the fights on the ground. It was lost at the strategic level."

Wynne's cheeks flushed with anger. "But Michael felt it was his duty to go," she said. "His duty..."

"Braver men than I refused to serve in Vietnam," said Jason quietly. "If Michael had taken this stand, too, he would still be alive." He reached toward her. "I'm sorry he was a casualty, Wynne..."

Wynne picked up a piece of pottery from the table, and threw it across the room. It crashed against the far wall, and broke into fragments that scattered to the floor.

"It just isn't fair!" she said.

"I know," Jason whispered. "Life isn't fair. It certainly isn't...to anyone."

He took her arm to steer her toward a chair.

Wynne wrenched free from Jason's hold, and ran from the work area to her office. She slammed the door and slid the bolt into place.

*Yes, it was true. Michael would still be alive if he had protested the war. If he refused to go. But that could never have been a consideration for him.* "We're making the world a better place to live," echoed in her thoughts.

*Would the agony of her loss ever end?* She took Michael's photograph in her hand. *It would not be in his nature to judge Jason's actions either. Her anger would have to remain hers alone.*

*How she could continue to work with Jason under the circumstances? Yet she needed a capable potter desperately to make the Gallery successful. Could they possibly have a completely professional relationship with no personal animosity spilling over?* She squared her shoulders, and realized she would have to try at least -- Shoreline Gallery's success very likely depended on it.

\*\*\*

WYNNE FELT SHE needed to talk with Jean. She stopped by the Stearns' home after leaving the Gallery, and picking up Stephen and Lauren at school. Jean was delighted to see them, and welcomed them with hugs. Stephen and Lauren hurried into the back yard to play on the swing set with Jon and Emily.

"What a nice surprise," Jean said as she poured two cups of coffee. "Will you stay and eat dinner with us?"

Wynne shook her head. "No, I just need to talk to you about Jason."

"Then he is a serial killer," Jean said with a gleam in her eye.

Wynne managed a smile, and thought wryly, *It might be a more acceptable label than war protester.*

"He's a war protester," Wynne finally revealed.

Jean almost broke her cup as it crashed to the saucer.

"A what?" she asked, her eyes widening.

"He protested against the war in Vietnam," Wynne said. "I've confronted him on it, but ..." Her voice trailed off and she didn't continue.

Jean's eyes were blazing. "Confronting is not the action you need to take. Wynne, fire him! We don't need a war protester in this community."

Wynne shook her head. "But his work is essential for the Gallery's success, Jean."

"Well, how successful do you think the Gallery will be if this military community finds out you're harboring a traitor?"

Wynne flinched. She had not thought of Jason as a traitor -- just as someone whose ideology was misplaced.

"I don't intend to advertise his stand on the war," Wynne said defensively. "And I'll hope you'll treat this conversation confidentially."

Jean's features softened, and she put her hand on Wynne's arm. "Of course I will. It's just that Michael gave his life for a war this guy protested."

"I know," Wynne said softly, putting her cup and saucer on the table, and standing to leave.

***

THE SETTING SUN radiated over the gulf when Wynne returned home. She watched the bands of light, and remembered the many early evening walks she and Michael had along the shore. As the waning sunlight flickered across the crest of the waves, she closed the shutters as though that would blot out the pain. The walks would now just be an ideal memory.

She made a cup of coffee, and sat on the sofa thinking about her talk with Jean. "We don't need a war protester in this community," Jean had said.

*How could she possibly justify having someone in her Gallery who had protested the war? She thought of Michael's patriotism, and how it never wavered despite the anti-war sentiment of many of the American people.* Though she found it hard to deny that we should never have been in Vietnam, she kept hearing Michael's voice saying, "But we're making the world a better place to live." He truly believed that!

Wynne put her head in her hands. She could not resolve her anger at Jason for protesting against a war Michael had died for -- or her anger at Michael for not coming home from that war.

## *Chapter Four*

*June, 1973*

AFTER HER DISCOVERY of Jason's earlier anti-war activities at the Republican National Convention, Wynne buried herself in work at the Gallery. Her mother was right -- "Your life now is your Gallery." She would therefore have to endure Jason because his pottery was so essential for the Gallery's success. And his carpentry skills rivaled his pottery ability. She vowed to maintain a working relationship despite her outrage at his actions. She tried to maintain a tone of civility when they had to speak.

Stephen and Lauren returned home after their visit with Mrs. Reardon. As soon as Wynne got them enrolled in their summer activities, the large mandala for Emerald Towers quickly took shape with her diligent efforts. It gave her an enormous sense of satisfaction as she filled the hoop with the brilliant yarns. *Perhaps I'll finish in time to attend the Art Show in Pensacola,* she mused as her fingers deftly wove the design on to the warp. The Art Show scheduled for June 10th in Pensacola was another invitational event where area artists displayed their work. She had attended for a number of years, and had a warm circle of friends in the group.

Placing the mandala on the work table, she went to her office to check her calendar. The piece was due in Miami on the same day as the Pensacola Art Show. She circled the date boldly -- "I'll make this one," she said aloud, and made a note to ship the mandala on June 5th.

Her mother telephoned later in the day. "Wynne, how are you? And the children?"

"We're fine, Mother...I'm busy on a commissioned piece."

"You are going to the annual event in Pensacola."

Wynne laughed inwardly. Her mother must have an internal calendar of all of the state's Art Shows.

"Yes, I am."

"Now don't let anything interfere, Wynne," she cautioned.

"No, Mother...I won't."

"You're sure there's no conflict with events at Eglin?"

Wynne felt a tightening in the pit of her stomach, and wished her mother would let it go.

"No...my calendar is clear."

"Good...I'll look forward to hearing about your weekend."

"Yes, I'll let you know..."

Wynne sighed and hung up the phone. She glanced at Michael's picture as she left the room.

Jason was holding the commissioned piece at arm's length when she went back to her work area. "Not bad," he said with a smile. "Let's celebrate with dinner out."

"I don't think so," Wynne said. "I'm on a rather tight schedule."

Jason took her by the arm. "Wynne, you may never be able to understand my position, but at least hear me out."

Wynne drew away and started working silently on the fiber piece.

Jason's brow furrowed as he turned to leave the room. "Perhaps another time," he said as he left.

Wynne put the fiber piece down on the worktable and angrily watched Jason leave. *How could she defile Michael's memory by even listening to someone's reasons for not defending his country? She wouldn't dignify Jason's excuses by listening. He had no defense to offer.*

\*\*\*

AFTER LEAVING STEPHEN and Lauren at the Stearns the next morning, Wynne decided to take the beach route along the Intracoastal Waterway to Pensacola for the Art Show. She sensed an uplifting feeling when she crossed the bridge at Navarre, and looked at the sunlight reflecting off the emerald blue waters of the sound. Sea oats bordered her route, their tall reeds reached for the sky from the crystal white sand dunes.

As she passed the contemporary designed cedar buildings bordering the Gulf Islands National Seashore, she recalled how she and Michael had joined in the battle to preserve this small section of beach from rampant condo development. It had been a difficult battle, but Michael's belief in the cause had never wavered. Their victory was primarily due to his determined commitment to save a portion of the natural seashore. They had celebrated with other involved friends when the government had set this piece of land aside for a permanent National Park.

She glanced at the pristine section of beach and thought wryly, *there is nothing in life that I can see or do that doesn't remind me of Michael. Would memories always bring sadness?* Feeling a twinge of guilt that remembrances of him were so difficult to bear, she pressed the accelerator hoping the Art Show would provide relief.

\*\*\*

CROWDS OF EXHIBITORS and visitors vied for parking places as Wynne circled the park where the Art Show would be held. She finally found a parking place one block away. Deciding to check out her display area before unpacking her car, she locked the car and walked quickly to the check-in booth.

"Wynne, how good to see you!"

Wynne turned and quickly received a bear hug from Janice Ryan, a fiber artist friend from years ago.

"Janice...how long has it been? Hawaii perhaps?"

"At least...did Michael come with you?"

Wynne felt a lump rising in her throat. *Of course, there would have been no way for Janice to know.* "No, he didn't..."

Her colleague, Lorraine Marshall, interrupted her. "Wynne, over here. Your booth is next to mine."

Wynne excused herself from Janice with a brief, "I'll talk with you later." She was relieved not to have to acknowledge Michael's death in this place she had sought out as a refuge.

Lorraine had already arranged her display of watercolors, mostly seascapes of the area. She walked to the car with Wynne, and helped her unload the fiber pieces.

"You've been a busy girl," she said, as she and Wynne carried a number of the fiber art tapestries.

"Yes, I have," Wynne admitted. "It helps. I like to stay busy."

"I know it's been hard," Lorraine said. "I only wish there were some way I could help."

*Would the specter of Michael's death ever end?* Wynne shook her head.

"No one can help, Lorraine. I have to get through this by myself."

They quickly displayed Wynne's fiber pieces on the frames that had been provided. The brightly colored yarns added a festive note to the entire area.

"Did Jason bring his pottery?" Lorraine asked.

"Yes...he should be here," Wynne said. "He planned to bring his truck, I believe."

Wynne looked at Lorraine's exhibit, and was pleased with her variety of seascapes. It should be a good day for Gallery sales.

She looked around the display area, but saw no sign of Jason. The day passed quickly for Wynne as visitors admired and bought many of her fiber pieces. She received orders to do five commissioned pieces, a record for her Art Show participation.

The Chaplain she met at the Gallery's Open House approached her booth.

"Mrs. Reardon, I believe," he said with a smile. "I would recognize your magnificent work anywhere."

Wynne smiled in appreciation, but could not take her eyes off the cross above his left shirt pocket as it glistened in the noonday sun. *How many times had he brought bad news to wives? What a sad duty.* She felt a sudden warmth and sympathy for this strong man.

"You do seem to enjoy art," she said.

"Yes, I'm truly a collector at heart," he agreed, fingering the yarn of her favorite nature tapestry. "I'll take this one," he said, reaching for his billfold.

"I believe you'll like that," Wynne replied. "It's one of...it's my favorite piece," she confided.

She wrapped the wall hanging in brown paper, and handed the package to him.

"I hope to see you again soon," he said.

"Yes, me, too," she replied, but regretted the hint of encouragement. The uniform, the cross, the square shouldered military bearing were too much for her.

The day that had such bright promise earlier quickly deteriorated as Wynne remembered the fun she and Michael had at previous Art Shows -- fun that would only be a memory now. Their trips were always a romantic encounter -- much like their honeymoon. When he was TDY, or couldn't get away, it just wasn't the same without him. But she had been determined to enjoy this one. It was her chance to enhance her new life -- her Gallery. And all it took to ruin the day was one look at a cross on a Chaplain's shirt.

The voice that broke her reverie was light-hearted, teasing.

"Business couldn't be that bad, Wynne," Jason said. "Smile!"

She was surprised that she welcomed the sight of him.

"Not bad at all," she replied.

"I see your nature tapestry is gone," he said, looking at the display area. "Hope it found a good home."

"A very good home," she said without further explanation, but the Chaplain's cross would not leave her thoughts.

"How about that dinner invitation you put on hold?" he asked. "I know this neat seafood restaurant on Pensacola Bay. Their gumbo recipe is a national treasure."

Wynne smiled nervously as Jason looked at her with an interest she found disturbing. If nothing else, Jason was indeed persistent. Yet perhaps a dinner out was just what she needed. She could at least be friendly since they had to work together. Anyway, she felt hungry after a day in the sun.

"Sounds good," she replied. "Let me pack up and we can go."

"Here, I'll help," he offered as he took down the remaining pieces. "Why don't I put them in my truck with my pottery?" he asked.

"Fine," she agreed, following him to the edge of the park where his familiar blue Chevy truck was parked.

***

AS THEY DROVE across Pensacola Bay, Wynne looked at the sailboats sailing in a regatta. Their multicolored spinnakers made a colorful spectacle against the cloudless sky as they raced the course.

"Looks like fun," Jason noted. "Do you sail?"

"Yes, Michael...that is we...yes, I have sailed," Wynne said. "It is fun."

Her thoughts returned to Hawaii, and their carefree days there when they sailed the beautiful waters of Waikiki. Michael was a master on a catamaran. She never quite got the hang of it, and deferred to his excellent sailing skills.

After they arrived and were seated at the Dolphin on the Bay Restaurant, Jason looked at the menu. "The gumbo is a requirement," he said. "Anything after that is just frosting on the cake."

Wynne ordered the gumbo reluctantly. "Anything one has to hide in a dark roux is not my idea of a gourmet dish," she said.

Jason laughed. "Now that's the most prejudiced thing I have ever heard about southern cooking."

Wynne laughed, too, and realized that it had only been when she was around Jason recently that she felt any sense of humor. There was something so entirely open and honest about him she felt a tendency truly to be herself, too.

"That's not prejudice," she defended. "It's a sense of preservation not wanting to eat some unknown denizen of the deep hiding in a roux."

"I give up," Jason said, throwing up his hands in mock despair.

After tasting it, Wynne had to admit the gumbo was outstanding; a blend of subtle spices, crabmeat, shrimp, fish, and okra with rice, and yes a dark brown roux.

"I stand corrected," she said with a smile after finishing the bowl. "It is very good."

"Am I ever wrong?" Jason asked, clasping her hand.   Wynne flinched and withdrew her hand. *Ever wrong?   How could she destroy the light-hearted moment with the reply that came so quickly to mind?*

"Perhaps, at times," she murmured simply. "Are you a native Californian?" she asked, realizing she knew nothing about Jason's family background.

"Yes," he said with some hesitation. "I grew up in Southern California."

"And your father is a master potter?" Wynne asked with a mischievous look.

"Hardly," Jason replied with a wry smile. "An economics professor at Stanford who believes the arts offer little contribution to the nation's economy. And my feelings about Vietnam...well," he said, shaking his head. "That's a whole other story."

"How about your family?" he asked.

"My father died five years ago," Wynne said, her voice catching on the words. "Mother lives in New Orleans and visits frequently."

They finished the meal with talk about the Art Show, and future plans for the Gallery.

Jason drove her back to the park after dinner to pick up her car. "See you tomorrow," he said with a smile.

"Tomorrow..." Wynne replied as she got into her car. She had enjoyed dinner with him and saw a side of him she hadn't seen before. There was apparently much more behind that gruff exterior that he tried to give to the world. Although she could never understand his view on the Vietnam War, she could perhaps understand and accept him as a fellow artist. *Maybe their alliance for the Gallery wouldn't be that bad after all.*

\*\*\*

IT HAD BEEN a busy week since the Art Show in Pensacola, and Wynne had the contented feeling all would be well with the Gallery. The responses for all of the pieces each Shoreline Gallery exhibitor had displayed at the Art Show had been excellent. They all were working diligently on additional commissioned pieces.

She totaled the month's receipts, and felt a warm glow of success inside. Maybe the Gallery would work after all. Income had exceeded expenses at last. She realized, too, that she had only thought of Michael once that day. In a sense it was a relief to know she had been so busy thoughts of him had been put aside. Yet she also felt a sense of guilt at her failure to think about him more that day.

The phone rang, breaking her reverie, as she entered the last figures.

"Shoreline Gallery."

"Wynne Reardon, please," a male voice requested.

"This is Wynne, may I help you?"

"I'm John Graves, a reporter for the" *Emerald Coast Gazette.* We would like to do a piece on you -- a profile of a Congressional Medal of Honor widow. May I make an appointment to see you soon?"

Wynne recoiled. *How could she go through all of that again for the media? And how could she not go through it for Michael's sake?*

She hesitated briefly. "Yes," she finally said. "I guess we could get together later this week."

"Fine. Is Friday at 10:00 a.m. at your Gallery all right?" he asked.

She looked at her calendar knowing already the date was open. "Yes, I'll see you then," she said, quickly writing the appointment on her calendar.

Wynne hung up the phone, and looked at Michael's picture. His smiling face comforted her and she blew him a kiss.

"I'll get through this somehow, Michael," she assured, turning off the light and leaving the room.

*\*\**

JOHN GRAVES ARRIVED promptly for the interview with a camera in his hand.

"I hope you don't mind," he said. "We would like to do a piece about you and your Gallery in conjunction with your being a Congressional Medal of Honor widow. Kind of what life is like for you now, and all of that..."

"Certainly," Wynne said. "I understand."

"Please tell me about Major Reardon," John said, looking at the picture on Wynne's desk. "Was he a career officer?"

"Yes," she said. "He had been in the Air Force for 15 years...we were married 13 years ago."

Graves jotted down his notes quickly.

"Could you explain the circumstances of his death, that is if it's not too painful, I mean? I'm sure our readers would like to know what happened. And why he was selected for the Congressional Medal of Honor?"

Wynne reached into her desk and pulled out the letter from General Arnold. She handed it to the reporter. "This explains the circumstances and the award," she said. "I don't think I can go into all of that again..."

"I understand," he said, quickly skimming the letter.

"You must be very proud of Major Reardon," he said, handing the letter back to her. "And what does the future hold for you now?"

"Well...the children...my Gallery...my fiber work," she said. "It is a full time job for me...not just a hobby."

"Yes, I've seen articles on the awards you've won state wide," he said with admiration. "Is there anything you can tell other widows that would help them, too?"

Wynne shook her head. "No," she said firmly. "It's an individual journey. I don't think anyone can give anyone else advice on how to get through it. Widowhood is a very personal thing."

"Certainly," he said. "That's a great quote." He wrote hastily in his notebook.

"Is there anything else?" Wynne asked, standing by her desk anxious to end the interview.

"No, I think I have everything I need. May I take some photographs now? Perhaps one of you standing in front of your wall-hangings, and a picture of the front of the Gallery."

"That would be fine," Wynne replied.

\*\*\*

THE SUNDAY LIFESTYLE section of the *Emerald Coast Gazette* headlined:

LOCAL CONGRESSIONAL MEDAL OF HONOR WIDOW AWARD WINNING ARTIST.

Wynne quickly skimmed the article. The reporter had written the circumstances of Michael's death and the Congressional Medal of Honor award quite accurately. The tone of the article indicated, however, she was coping extremely well with her loss by devoting her energies to the Gallery. The Gallery and her children were hardly a replacement for Michael, but it was all she had. Perhaps she should not fault the reporter for his erroneous assumption. The world -- at least her circle of friends it seemed -- felt she was coping quite well. If this deception made them feel better, perhaps it was for the best.

## Chapter Five

*July, 1973*

"LOOK, MAMA, IT'S Daddy!" Lauren exclaimed.

Wynne's heart leapt at the sight of the Air Force officer standing ramrod straight by her door, as she and the children arrived home from an evening event at the Gallery. Her foot jammed the brake, then relaxed and allowed the car to roll to a gentle stop at the garage.

"No, darling," she said breathlessly. "It's not Daddy. It's someone...else." Her knees were weak when she got out of the car and opened the children's door.

"I don't want someone," Lauren whined. "I want Daddy."

"Sh-h-h." Wynne paused for control before turning to face the officer who came toward her now, his expression somber.

"Mrs. Reardon?"

"Yes."

"I'm Tom Markham, Michael's wingman."

Wynne caught her breath. *He would know what happened. He was there!*

"Oh, Tom. How nice to meet you. Michael told me so much about you." She shook his hand warmly. "Please come in...and do call me Wynne."

"Tom, this is Stephen and Lauren," she said as they entered the house. "Are you a pilot like Dad?" Stephen asked.

Tom's eyes glistened. "Yes, I was your Dad's wingman."

"OK, you two. Off to bed," their mother encouraged.

"Goodnight, Sir," Stephen said.

"Goodnight, Young Fellow."

Tom sat on the edge of Michael's stuffed lounge chair, fingering the fold of his hat. His blue eyes clouded as he spoke. A shock of unruly blonde hair on his forehead gave him an almost boyish appearance.

"Wynne, I wish I could bring you better news," he said, lowering his eyes. "Colonel Rutledge asked me to talk with you."

Wynne couldn't speak. She held up her hands, urging him to stop – she didn't want to hear – but he continued to look down, missing her signal.

"I know that you're reluctant to accept Michael's death. We thought perhaps if I talked to you...about what I saw, I mean...you could understand the circumstances better."

Wynne felt a quickening in the pit of her stomach. *What could Tom possibly tell her that the Casualty Office and Ray hadn't already revealed?*

As if from a distance she heard herself say, "Please go on, Tom."

"I sighted Michael and his parachute the day he was forced to eject from his plane. He was caught in the shroud lines that were snarled in a tree...there was no movement – nothing to indicate he was alive. He never responded to any of our communications, but we could hear his beeper..." Tom paused as though he were gathering his thoughts. He then continued, "There was so much hostile fire we couldn't get Rescue in and night was coming on. Next morning and for several days reconnaissance helicopter flew over and took photographs. They had me review the pictures. Wynne, he hadn't moved. The attitude of the body...Well, experts are convinced beyond a doubt that he was dead."

She held up her hands to stop him. *No, just unconscious, maybe. Not dead. How could they be sure? They just took pictures. Could they see his face? Maybe it wasn't Michael. It was someone else.*

She was on her feet. She couldn't stop the torrent of denials that poured from her lips until she felt the young Captain's firm hands on her shoulders. "Wynne, there was a brisk wind blowing. His arms and legs were unyielding, the body was rigid. I'm sorry to have to say this. Michael is dead."

All resistance went out of Wynne. The world she knew ended. And it had to be the end of her denial of the truth. She must face the fact that Michael would not be coming home. *Ever.*

"I'm sorry I have made this so difficult for you," she said, feeling as though someone else were speaking.

Tom reached out and held her in a comforting embrace. "Michael was a great guy. He could fly that bird better than anyone else...I only wish that he..." There seemed to be something else he wanted to reveal, but instead he turned to leave.

"Yes he was," she said softly, walking with Tom to the door. "Yes he was..."

He stopped at the door, and put his hand gently on her shoulder. "I have Michael's things...whenever you're ready."

Wynne nodded and said, "Thank you for coming...I know how hard this has been for you, too."

After Tom left, she closed the door and covered her face with her hands. *Why Michael?* It seemed so unfair to die in a war that was not even supported by the American people. He had written when he first went to Southeast Asia that he had been trained to fight the enemy. But he had found the enemy in Vietnam was so undefined. *Oh, God, how could something undefined have killed the person she loved? They had so many plans, so many dreams...*

She walked to the telephone, and dialed the Casualty Office's number from memory. "This is Wynne Reardon. I'd like to schedule a Memorial Service for my husband, Major Michael Reardon, as soon as possible...Yes, Eglin Chapel...Tuesday, July 17th...at ten will be fine."

She then dialed her mother's number, and fought back tears as she heard her mother's voice.

"Mother, the news about Michael isn't good...he is presumed dead. The Memorial Service is scheduled for Tuesday, July 17th, at ten. I hope you can come."

She heard her mother crying at the other end of the line.

"Oh, darling, I'm so sorry...of course I'll be there. I'll take the next flight..."

Wynne made a similar call to Michael's mother. A Casualty Notification Officer had already delivered the report from General Arnold. After a brief tearful conversation, Wynne said simply, "I'll see you Tuesday."

Wynne then went to Stephen's room, and stopped momentarily to watch his peaceful sleep. She would wait until morning to tell the children.

She called Jason and told him about the ceremony. "Yes," she said softly. "I would like for you to attend."

\*\*\*

*July 17, 1973*

AS SHE WATCHED the F-4 jets streak across the cloudless Florida sky, Wynne shielded her eyes from the glare of the sun. An audible gasp came from the crowd as one of the jets pulled out of the close formation, and climbed out of sight into the heavens leaving a vacant slot. Sadness etched her face as she watched the missing man formation pay final tribute to Major Michael Reardon. Stephen and Lauren sobbed as Chaplain Turner put his comforting arms around them.

Beside her, Michael's mother wept aloud while Wynne's mother held tightly to her daughter's hand. Wynne flinched at the 21-gun salute, and was overwhelmed with sadness as the haunting sound of *Taps* echoed across the Florida landscape.

It was not Wynne's first Memorial Service by any means. She had remarked to Michael just last year that when you have attended 15 Memorial Services for friends by the time you are 35 there is something definitely wrong with our world.

"We're making the world a better place to live," he said with his usual optimism. From someone else it might have sounded trite, but Michael was a believer.

A better place to live...dear Michael. He truly believed that. His patriotism never wavered, even

91

in the Vietnam controversy. He had joined his country's stand against communism, and had lost his life.

As the jets disappeared from view, Wynne felt an arm around her shoulder, a gentle squeeze.

"Wynne, we're as close as the telephone if you need us."

Wynne turned to face their friends, Jean and Ray Stearns. Ray had been in flight school with Michael, and Jean had been Wynne's friend and confidante through all of the moves and long separations.

She clasped Jean's hand. "I know you are...thank you."

She struggled to keep her composure through all of the expressions of condolences. Of course, everyone had promised they would always be there for her. Her parents certainly had. She recalled her mother's brave smile as Wynne and Michael boarded the plane for their tour in London.

"We can come if you need us," her mother had said, hugging her daughter warmly. Her father died in a car accident while she and Michael were stationed in England. The loss of her father had been devastating, and then there was the near loss of the baby...

Remembrances of her pregnancy flooded back. They had been stationed at Clark Field in the Philippines in 1966 when she found out she was expecting their first child. Michael was overjoyed at the prospect of being a father. He had told the entire squadron before she could even call her mother with the news.

"The Miami Dolphins will have another star quarterback in the 1990s", he said proudly, never doubting for a moment that the baby would be a boy.

"That'll be another step for women's lib," she teased. "The first female quarterback in professional football history!"

Their excitement over the impending addition to the Reardon family pervaded the entire squadron. Wagers on date of birth, whether girl or boy, and time of delivery began to circulate among Michael's fellow pilots shortly after the announcement the Reardons would be parents.

*** 

WYNNE WAS IN a state of euphoria as she planned to turn their tiny second bedroom in base housing into a nursery. Michael would paint the walls a pale yellow, and she began refinishing the furniture in white -- a chest, a rocker, and a crib that had been hers as a baby were sent over by her mother for Elizabeth Carmichael's first grandchild.

Wynne lovingly stripped the paint from each piece, and spent weeks carefully repainting them. Michael cautioned her about overdoing as she entered her eighth month of the pregnancy, but she assured him she was pacing herself.

He was away on a mission the day she started having contractions. She didn't think much about the discomfort at first, but on the second day, the pain was too severe to ignore. Her neighbor happened to stop in for coffee, and found Wynne crumpled on the floor. She was rushed to the base hospital where Stephen was born one month prematurely on October 16th. Stephen, like his father, came into the world as a fighter. He struggled for weeks to overcome a lung problem caused by the premature birth, but he fought it and thrived. They were ecstatic two years later with Lauren's birth on October 11, 1968.

She had almost lost a part of Michael with Stephen's premature birth. Now she had lost Michael.

"Wynne, how good to see you again...I mean...I'm so sorry it has to be under these circumstances." Rachel Andrews was ill at ease, uncertain what to say, as were so many of their friends at the Memorial Service.

Rachel's husband Ron stood by her side with the same inspiring military bearing that had distinguished Michael. They had been stationed at Hickam Field together during Michael's first overseas tour.

"Thank you for coming," Wynne said hugging her friend.

"Please call us...if there's anything..." Rachel dabbed at her eyes with her handkerchief. She hugged Wynne's mother and Mrs. Reardon.

Connie and her husband John expressed their sympathy, too. "We want to help...do let us know..."

Others whom they had known at bases all over the world also paid their respects. What a remarkable network of communication existed between military friends, and Michael had many friends. Condolences poured in -- telephone calls and cards, potted plants -- even a tree to plant in his memory -- and now all these friends pressing around her. Michael's former Squadron Group

Commander from Hickam Field, Colonel Ted Jefferies, shook her hand and offered condolences. Squadron members, whose names she couldn't even remember, expressed their sympathy, and encouraged her to call if they could be of any help.

"You could bring Michael back to me!" she wanted to cry out, but dared not.

*Thank God Michael can't see my reaction now.* She muffled a sob. But surely he wouldn't expect her to be stoic and dry-eyed through this service or in the days and nights still to come.

Jason approached her, took her hand, and said, "Wynne, I'm very sorry."

His brown eyes reflected a deep sense of concern.

"Thank you," she said as Jean asked, "Shall we go now?"

As Wynne held the neatly folded American flag in her arms, Ray took her arm, and guided her to the car while Jean escorted Stephen and Lauren. Only a handful of people remained on the grassy hill, talking quietly. An American flag, flying at half-mast, fluttered in the breeze on the podium. An Honor Guard stood stiffly at attention beneath the flag, their medals and rifles reflecting the rays of the sun.

***

WYNNE'S MOTHER AND Mrs. Reardon stayed for several days. Their grief was suffocating for Wynne -- she could hardly deal with her own much less buoy up anyone else's spirits. She wasn't much help to Stephen and Lauren, who seemed bewildered by all the expressions of emotion. Mrs. Reardon especially seemed to be in a world of grief all her own. Wynne managed the perfunctory "thank you" as friends visited, but it was impossible to engage her in conversation. Her mother appeared compelled to take over for the both of them. Mrs. Carmichael's incessant advice and pronouncements often fell on deaf ears, but she persisted undeterred in her role as caretaker.

As well-meaning as they both had been to be with her, it was still a relief when her mother and Estelle Reardon both left for their respective homes. Wynne would probably never forget the look of despair in Mrs. Reardon's eyes as she told her good-bye at the airport. Even Stephen and Lauren, who had been a delight through the years for their grandmother, could not capture her attention. They both hugged her as she started down the corridor to her plane, but she hardly seemed aware of their good-byes.

Wynne returned home after the tearful partings at the airport. How quiet the house was with her mother and Mrs. Reardon gone. Thoughtful neighbors and friends entertained Stephen and Lauren daily. She welcomed the stillness. As the sun slipped below the horizon and disappeared into the Gulf of Mexico, she adjusted the shutters in her home studio. She stood at the window watching the hues of fading sunlight rippling over the crest of the waves. The setting sun blurred her view of the lone sailboat slipping now through the crimson water. Shivering from the cool sea breeze, she pulled her sweater across her shoulders and latched the shutters.

How Michael had loved sailing! She remembered the many sunsets they had shared. As Wynne had watched the sun slip below the horizon, she pictured his tall figure on the beach with the erect military bearing, even in his swimsuit. She loved the way the sea breezes ruffled his blonde hair giving it a feathery appearance. She smiled as she realized his ruffled hair was the only feature that belied his crisp military bearing. Her body quivered as she remembered his tender caresses. How she longed for that touch!

Other memories of his subsequent assignment at Hickam Air Force Base in Hawaii flooded back, and she recalled the sunsets at Waimea Bay on the North Shore of Oahu. She'd had to remind herself often then they were not on a permanent vacation. They spent his off-duty hours at the beach where they sailed, swam, and snorkeled in the emerald waters. As evening approached, they would often picnic, and watch the sun sink on the horizon. The giant orange ball somehow seemed larger over the vast expanse of the Pacific Ocean.

Wynne had used the scene in many of her wall hangings. The brilliant hues of orange and yellow changing to purple as darkness settled provided a natural palette, and array of colors that she reproduced with yarns. Her award-winning pieces hung in many galleries.

Yet those carefree early years had hardly prepared her for his assignments -- the dangerous fighter pilot duty and the long absences. But the memories of their tour in Hawaii were everlasting. On their first Thanksgiving together -- others had been apart -- they vacationed in a little rented cottage at Bellows Beach near Hickam Field. Michael had smoked a turkey, and they had celebrated with friends. Their home was always the gathering place for the squadron. The assignment in Hawaii brought many pleasing memories of Stephen and Lauren's toddler years. Their presence helped Wynne through Michael's many temporary duty trips away from home.

And now the Reardons had come full circle -- back to where his first assignment had brought them as newlyweds after his flight training. She recalled another fly-over when Michael received his commission. She had proudly pinned the wings on his chest. *How many moves ago had it been? She had lost count after four.*

Wynne always took the news of a transfer well. It wasn't easy to leave a familiar place and good friends, but buoyed by his confidence and optimism she approached each move as an adventure. She had little patience for military wives who constantly complained about moving.

"Ron told me today that he wished some of your enthusiasm about transfers would rub off on Rachel," Michael had said. "She's giving him a fit about moving to Germany. As though he has a choice!"

Some of the wives even teased her about it. At the Hail and Farewell coffees, she'd often hear someone way, "Too bad this isn't for Wynne. She loves to move."

Well, in reality she didn't love to move. But his career meant everything to her. And if moving would advance his career, then moving was an opportunity. She took the teasing good-naturedly and detected certain envy in their voices. "You're a good sport," Michael often told her, flashing that wide smile that never failed to quicken her heart.

***

NOW THE TRANSFERS and new duty assignments were over. The house at 234 Gulf View Lane would be her permanent home. It was the waterfront home they had dreamed about and saved for over the years, and where they looked forward to retirement, watching sunsets over the Gulf of Mexico. They bought the home and through ensuing assignments rented the house to military friends with the understanding the Reardons would eventually return there to live some day. Some day had come for Wynne. Now she would put down roots here for her and the children without Michael.

The cedar-sided contemporary structure blended well into the pine tree shaded lot. The sleek lines of the house reached skyward, framed by the silhouettes of the pines. Michael had nursed the trees from saplings on his infrequent trips back to

Florida. His last admonition to tenants had always been, "Keep the trees well watered!", knowing all along the irrigation system he had so meticulously installed would do the job for them. And now the trees towered over the dwelling providing ample shade from the bright Florida sun.

\*\*\*

SHE RECEIVED A call from her secretary on Friday. "Wynne, it's Connie. Could I come by to talk with you about the order for supplies for the Randolph piece? I have a million questions."

Wynne smiled. Her compulsive Gallery worker would worry both of them into a state before they finished the commissioned piece for the Randolph Museum.

"Sure. Right now okay?"

"That's perfect. I'll be right over."

Wynne put on a pot of coffee, and sliced some pound cake. She welcomed Connie's visit, even with her friend's anxiety about the Randolph piece. As much as she had looked forward to her mother and Mrs. Reardon leaving after the Memorial

Service, she had felt terribly alone and very sad since their departure.

She answered the doorbell, and found Connie holding a sheaf of papers, her face flushed.

"Thanks for letting me come," Connie said breathlessly. "I can't have you miss the deadline because I failed to order supplies in time."

Wynne smiled ruefully. If they missed the date of completion, it would probably be due to her lack of motivation, not Connie's failure to order materials. Besides, her colleague's compulsive efficiency was legendary.

Putting a calming hand on Connie's shoulder, Wynne assured, "Don't worry about the deadline -- we'll make it!"

Connie nodded and sat on a stool at the kitchen counter while Wynne served the coffee and cake.

"How are you, Wynne?" Connie asked softly.

"I'm fine," Wynne said, patting Connie's hand. "Really..."

The word, fine, seemed to come out of Wynne's mouth like a programmed response when friends asked about her well-being. What was she to reply, "I'm not doing very well, thank you."? Her friends surely didn't want to hear that.

"That's good," Connie said, sipping her coffee. "I don't know how I could..." Her voice trailed off, and she turned her face away.

Quickly regaining her composure, she handed Wynne a Gallery requisition form.

"Here's the order," she said.

Wynne scanned the list. Connie, as usual, had exactly every item needed for the piece listed correctly. Wynne took a pen from a mug on the counter, and signed the request. "Thanks, Connie," she said. "How would I manage without you?"

They finished their cake and coffee with little more conversation. When Wynne walked her friend to the door, Connie said, "I'll mail this tomorrow."

Wynne nodded and closed the door. *Tomorrow. There was always another tomorrow -- just like today.* The routine of each day had not been too different since Michael's death because he was frequently on long TDYs. During these absences, she had lived for the time he would be home again. Now there was little to look forward to. Her daily routine had not changed significantly -- only her motivation. Now she struggled to get through each day.

She took the partially completed mandala from her worktable, and held it over the mantelpiece hoping to renew her interest in its completion. Wynne put the hoop back on the table. *Perhaps I will finish it later.* She paused in front of the unopened letter leaning against the frame with his photograph. He would speak to her through this letter one more time, and so he was not really dead until...She read Michael's neat script on the envelope, *Mrs. Michael Reardon.*

*That's who I am and will always be.* She blew her nightly kiss at his picture before turning out the light, and heading for her bedroom for another lonely night. How she missed and longed for his presence in her bed. She wanted to be able to turn over, and touch his hair and his hand. *It was an aching and longing that she feared would never cease.*

## Chapter Six

*August, 1973*

WYNNE AWOKE WITH the sun streaming through the louvered shutters. Seagulls cried noisily from the beach as they searched the glistening sand for their morning meal.

Groggily she reached for Michael's terry cloth bathrobe, her security blanket against these lonely mornings. She felt numb and alone wrapped in his blue paid robe that fitted her like a tent. It still smelled faintly of his aftershave and cologne. Helplessly, she clinched her fists inside the long sleeves.

"How could you leave me?" she shouted, and instantly felt guilty at her anger. Anger at Michael, at their well-meaning friends, and yes, even her mother.

No one could understand the depth of her grief. How dare they say, "I know how you feel,

Wynne." How could anyone know how she felt -- how destitute and insecure about the future? Her grief was not only for his death, but also for the end of the marvelous life she had shared with him -- his warm, compassionate love that made her life full. And now she was a widow. *Widow.* The word reverberated through her thoughts. Such an empty, heartless term. It sounded like a lifetime sentence with Colonel Rutledge imposing the judgment: "Mrs. Michael Reardon, you are now declared a widow."

*How long will I have to keep up this stoic facade for Mother, Michael's family, and my friends?* She wished she could rail out at God for letting it happen, or to Michael for not coming home, or to family and friends who could never understand her feelings.

She felt as though she had been detached from the whole experience -- sitting somewhere apart watching herself in a scene doing all the right things -- the plastic smiles, the demure 'thank you's, the mechanical greetings as though her feelings had been turned off. But this proper image shattered when she was alone. Any remembrance of him sent a wave of grief over her. It hurt so much to think about him. Yet how could she feel this way when his actual presence had given her such happiness?

Such thoughts unleashed feelings of guilt and she was on a roller coaster ride of grief and guilt with any remembrance of Michael.

Her red swollen eyes stared back at her from the mirror, sending a tremor over her. She would need to repair the damage before waking the children. After that she must keep an appointment at the Personnel Office regarding her military benefits. She shuddered at the thought. *How could someone's life be defined in monetary value anyway?* But financial reality was indeed a fact she had to face now. She called Stephen and Lauren to breakfast.

Lauren rubbed her eyes as she crawled up on the stool at the kitchen counter. "Can we have pancakes?" she asked.

Stephen followed quickly behind her. "Can we, Mom?"

"I'm sorry, Darling. I have an appointment. It'll have to be cereal this morning."

"O. K.," Lauren said as Wynne poured two bowls of cereal, and put a pitcher of milk on the table.

"Where's the appointment, Mom?" Stephen asked as he ate his cereal.

"It's at the base...I have to settle Dad's finances," Wynne explained.

"What's finances?" Lauren asked. She wiped milk from her chin.

"It's money," Stephen explained.

"It's about Dad's life insurance...and our medical insurance," Wynne added.

She quickly showered and dressed. After grabbing a quick cup of coffee, she took Stephen and Lauren next door to stay with their neighbor. "See you this afternoon!" she said with forced enthusiasm.

It was a beautiful August day -- so typical of late summer on the Gulf coast. Sunlight sparkled off the crest of the waves as she drove along Gulf View Lane. Sea oats fluttered in the breeze, their tall stalks resiliently bending to touch the sand dunes, and then springing back upright. It was an idyllic scene -- one she and Michael had often enjoyed during their strolls on the beach. For a fleeting moment, she imagined she was simply picking Michael up for a picnic lunch at their favorite cove.

The guard at Eglin Air Force Base waved her through the gate with a snappy salute when he saw the officer's sticker on the car's bumper. She parked at the Administration Building, and entered the lobby where an airman at the information desk pointed the way to the Personnel Office. There Wynne found Major Ralph Harrison waiting for her.

"Mrs. Reardon, how nice to meet you. Please come in," he said, leading her to a room filled with files. "All we need is your signature on some forms, and they can be processed immediately. We already have the death certificate."

Wynne recoiled. The term death certificate went through her like a shaft of ice. She could hardly bring herself to even pronounce the word, death, much less deal with its reality yet.

Major Harrison continued, "You will receive six months gratuity pay plus the value of Major Reardon's life insurance policy. The policy comes to $50,000. A check will be mailed to you in about four weeks. If you should need an advance sooner than that, we can arrange it."

Wynne shook her head. "I'll be fine for that long."

"There are a number of suggestions our office makes which may help you with this transition," Major Harrison said.

*Transition? Widowhood is more than a transition. It's an end to all I've known...*

"Let's review this list," he said, calling her attention back to a typed sheet that he held in his hand. "First, you need to locate records on where all your bank and investment accounts are. Do you know where these records are kept?"

"Yes," Wynne replied. "I've handled all of our finances while Michael's been away."

"That's good...You'll need to provide a death certificate for each account to remove your husband's name, and the requirement for his signature on subsequent transactions. Do you have any credit cards in your name? I mean as Wynne Reardon, not Mrs. Michael Reardon?"

Wynne felt a knot in the pit of her stomach. *It seemed she had always been Mrs. Michael Reardon. Did she have to give that up?*

"No, I don't," she admitted, trying to focus her thoughts on the Major's question. "All my cards are as Mrs. Michael Reardon."

"Well, you need to change that immediately," Major Harrison said rather brusquely. "It's important for you to establish credit in your name. Your medical coverage through Champus and that for Stephen and Lauren will continue. You retain commissary and BX privileges, which may be a consideration in any plans to relocate. A military installation nearby can be a great advantage," he explained.

Not living close to a military base had ever crossed Wynne's mind. She couldn't imagine moving away from this place Michael had loved and the home they had shared. Wynne only nodded, and the officer continued.

"Major Reardon may have had other life insurance policies besides the government policy we talked about...but not necessarily. Fighter pilots are rather high risk. However, you should look into it. Perhaps in a safe deposit box?

Our office can supply whatever copies of the death certificate you need to make claims against any other policies he may have," he assured. "Did he have a will?"

"Yes," Wynne said. "We attended a program through Family Services during our first assignment. They explained the importance of having a will."

"Well, that's good," Major Harrison said. "I would recommend also that you get in touch with an investment counselor."

"I will," Wynne assured. "Is there anything else?"

"No, I believe this will do it after you sign these forms...please call our office if we can be of any further assistance. Meanwhile I will be calling from time to time, if I may, just to be sure things are going well."

Wynne signed the documents with an unsteady hand, and thanked the officer for his help. An overwhelming feeling of emptiness overcame her as she walked out of the building, a widow with two children and a future she could not imagine.

She drove out of the base in a haze of tears. There could be no more denial -- "Our office can supply whatever copies of the death certificate you need," echoed in her thoughts. She must erase his name from their financial accounts. *Michael was dead*.

She turned on to Beach View Lane, and pulled into a parking lot to look at the seascape that always gave her such a sense of peace. The vast panorama of the Gulf of Mexico stretched before her as she looked across the brilliant sugar-white beach. A seagull flew gracefully over the breaking waves, its feathers almost touching the frothing surf.

"I can do that," Michael used to say, watching the gulls, and he'd describe an aerial maneuver to her with his hands like wings.

*Oh, God, this isn't the future I wanted.* She stared at the rolling surf. She could see Michael strolling this same beach, tossing unbleached sand dollars back into the Gulf on the outside chance they might still be alive. "A dollar saved is a dollar earned," he would paraphrase with his wide grin. He strode into her thoughts -- the golden tan of his hard sturdy body highlighting his blonde hair and blue eyes. Those eyes that could pierce your very soul, and yet dance with laughter at a moment's notice.

Her arms ached to hold him...The cry of a seagull, like the creak of a rusty hinge, broke her reverie, and she found herself weeping, the grief she had kept inside for weeks finally unleashed. Away from the eyes of her children, her mother, Jean, or Colonel Rutledge she was free to let all the sadness and anger pour out.

When the body wrenching sobs finally stopped, Wynne wiped her face with a tissue. After regaining her composure, she slipped off her sandals and walked down to the water's edge where the foaming surf danced around her feet.

Sunlight glinted off the emerald green water, but the radiance failed to warm her.

A lone sandpiper, scurrying along the edge of the foaming surf, pecked frantically at shells the tide brought in. *How mindlessly it follows its instincts to survive. In that moment she realized she did not want to go on living, but she could not give up the daily efforts to survive, because her children needed her.*

Her future -- their future -- had been reduced to a day-by-day agenda of clerical tasks related to his death. She resolved to see them done, and walked back to her car. The sandpiper scurried back to the water's edge, still alone.

When Wynne arrived home, she found an official looking letter in her mailbox. She quickly opened and read the contents.

*Dear Mrs. Reardon:*

*This letter is an invitation for you to attend the Congressional Medal of Honor ceremony at the White House on Thursday, 23 August, 1973, at 1100 hours. At that time President Nixon will award our nation's highest medal for valor, posthumously, to Major Michael James Reardon in recognition of his effort for his country above and beyond the call of duty.*

*Colonel Rutledge's office will provide transportation for you, the children, and Captain Tom Markham whom we've asked to accompany you to Washington.*

*Arrangements have been made for you and Major Reardon's mother to stay at the guest quarters at Andrews Air Force base. Please contact my office if we can be of any further assistance.*

*Sincerely,*

*Justin Burroughs*

*U.S. House of Representatives*

*Congressional District 1, FL*

Wynne pressed the letter to her heart. How proud Michael would be of his honor! If only he could be here to receive it. *Posthumously.* She liked the word even less than *widow*, but they were both a part of her vocabulary -- of her identity now.

When Stephen and Lauren arrived home from school, Wynne explained the Congressional Medal of Honor award to them. "You mean the President of the United States will give you a medal for Dad" Stephen asked wide-eyed. "That's cool!"

"Can we go?" Lauren asked, her eyes dancing with excitement.

"Of course," Wynne said with hugs for both of them. "Grandmother Reardon will be there, too."

Wynne went into the Gallery the next day, and explained her plans to go to Washington to Jason.

"A Congressional Medal of Honor...that's quite a commendation," he said.

"Then you can cover the Gallery while I'm gone?"

"Of course," he assured.

"Thanks," she murmured and then went into her office.

"Hello, anyone here?" her friend Jean asked from the hallway.

"Inside my office," Wynne called out.

Jean popped her head in the door. "There you are! I've looked everywhere for you. I assumed you'd be putting up displays in the showroom," she said with a smile.

"No, just going through my mail," Wynne replied. "I don't know if I'll ever see the end of letters from friends. Michael had so many..." She held up the batch of letters that had just arrived.

"I know," Jean said softly, putting a hand on her shoulder. "And how is Wynne today?"

Wynne smiled slightly. "Fine, I guess...trying to get everything finished so the children and I can go to Washington next week. The ceremony is the 23rd. His mother will meet me there, and Colonel Rutledge has asked Tom Markham to go with me."

"I'm glad you aren't going without a military escort," Jean said. "But I'm not sure I would want to go with Tom."

Wynne looked surprised. "Why not Tom? He was Michael's friend and wingman."

"I know," Jean said. "But his reputation bothers me."

"What about his reputation?" Wynne asked. "From all Michael had ever said about Tom, he was the perfect pilot."

"Well, Ray says he's always trying to do the fastest turn, the neatest roll, and take credit for all of the successful missions," Jean said. "A bit of a show-off if you ask me," she said with a shrug.

"Surely not," Wynne said. "Michael believed he was a good pilot."

"Now, Wynne, did you ever hear Michael say anything bad about anyone?" Jean asked. "Certainly not one of his flight members."

Wynne had to admit Michael was not one to criticize anyone else. Especially where his career might be affected. But the thought crossed her mind momentarily. *What was Tom doing when he was supposed to be protecting Michael's bombing mission? Was he hot-dogging his plane then?* It was a thought she couldn't dwell on, and dismissed it from her mind.

"Oh, well. I guess he will be a capable escort," Jean admitted. "He'll probably regale you with stories of his heroic missions. Tell me about your plans...when do you leave?"

"Colonel Rutledge will provide a flight from Eglin. We'll leave at 4:00 p.m. on Wednesday. The ceremony is eleven on Thursday morning. Michael's mother will meet us there. I know this will be a hard trip for her, too." Wynne remembered the haunting look in his mother's eyes when they had parted after the Memorial Service.

"You must be so proud of Michael," Jean said. "Imagine a Congressional Medal of Honor!"

"Yes," Wynne said. "He would be proud, too."

\*\*\*

WYNNE CHOSE A navy blue tailored dress, trimmed in white, with navy shoes for the ceremony. She held the dress to her, and surveyed her appearance in the mirror above her dresser. Her hazel eyes reflected back sadness she could not dispel, making her look much older than her 35 years. As she carefully folded the dress and placed it in her luggage, she looked at the picture of Michael on her bureau. His smiling eyes seemed to say, "It's okay, I'll be there with you." She blew him a kiss and closed the bag.

She then packed a bag for Stephen and Lauren. As she held up Stephen's navy blue suit, she knew how proud Michael would be of their young man. And Lauren would look like an angel in her white dotted Swiss dress. She packed the clothes, and gently closed the lid on their luggage.

\*\*\*

TOM MARKHAM MET them at the flight line as the 707 warmed up on the runway. He took the bags from her, and linked his arm in hers as they walked to the plane. Stephen and Lauren followed closely behind.

"I'm glad I was invited to go with you and the children, Wynne," Tom said. "It seems like the last thing I could do for Michael."

Wynne winced. *Was this the last thing Tom could have done? Or could he have found Michael sooner if he had been paying proper attention to his flying. Or was he the one who was out of his sector?* She probably would never know, but the questions lingered.

The flight attendant helped Stephen and Lauren get settled in their seats.

As the plane took off and circled over the Gulf of Mexico, Wynne saw the sunlight glinting off the crest of the waves again with the same radiance she had seen earlier. She did not feel any similar radiance in her life just now. She sighed and looked at one of the magazines she'd brought to read as the plane veered northward toward Washington, D.C.

"What was it like, Tom?" she asked, looking up from her magazine.

"Like?" Tom replied with a puzzled look on his face.

"I mean when you were searching for Michael?"

"We flew over the area of his mission until we found his parachute...it was easily visible from our altitude."

"But how could you be so sure it was his parachute?" Wynne asked.

"His plane was the only one to go down in that area, Wynne...there's no doubt. I saw him bail out." He took her hand and squeezed it gently. "Wynne, I would give the world if you were right -- that it wasn't Michael -- that I could have that day back and do it better. I was his wingman. We feel so responsible for each other. But Michael's dead. I saw him...you have to accept that..."

Wynne looked out the plane window at the small images below. *Is that what Michael looked like? Just a small dot near the Vietnamese hillside?*

The pain of her loss was suffocating as she remembered him...football captain...first in his class in flight school...her first date in college, a blind date whose blue eyes and warm smile won her heart immediately.

She looked back at Tom, but he was looking straight ahead, absorbed in his own thoughts. Picking up her magazine again, she thumbed through it, but it was impossible to focus on any of the material. *Would she ever know for sure what had happened on that mission? Had someone been at fault? Who?*

As the plane circled over Washington, D.C., Wynne looked out her window at the landmarks. She saw the well-planned design spread out on the Maryland side of the Potomac River. Wynne pointed out the landmarks to Stephen and Lauren. The needle-like Washington monument rose majestically skyward, while the White House, the Capitol, the Lincoln and Jefferson Memorials formed a cross centering on the monument. Sun glinted off the capitol's cast iron dome, and she could see the ribbon-like Arlington Memorial Bridge spanning the Potomac and running in a straight line to Arlington Cemetery.

*If only Michael's body could have been recovered, he could have been buried there. But there was no body -- only a memory.* She turned in her seat to get a last glimpse of the cemetery as the plane banked to come in for a landing.

After the pilot made a flawless landing of the 707, Tom observed, "Safe and conservative."

As the plane taxied into the terminal, passengers were advised to remain seated, until priority passengers deplaned. A smiling flight attendant approached Wynne and escorted her, Stephen, Lauren, and Captain Markham to a waiting staff car.

"Mrs. Reardon, I'm Matthew Holmes," said the Colonel, waiting beside the car. "We have your quarters ready." He shook her hand warmly and helped them into the car.

Captain Markham saluted smartly, "Captain Markham, Sir!" he said in proper clipped voice, and climbed in the front seat next to the uniformed driver.

"Your husband's mother will arrive early tomorrow," the Colonel said. He briefed her gently on the schedule, but she had difficulty concentrating.

"I have it all on my schedule, Wynne. Don't worry," Tom assured.

Wynne nodded and silently watched the activity on the flight line as the driver took them to base billeting. Stephen pressed his nose against the window, and watched the planes being serviced, asking questions which Tom answered patiently. At base billeting they were given a charming suite in the Visiting Officer's Quarters, adjoining the suite reserved for her mother-in-law. Captain Markham's quarters were down the hall.

\*\*\*

WYNNE AWOKE EARLY the next morning, helped the children dress and then showered. She dressed to have breakfast with Mrs. Reardon. She dreaded facing Michael's mother again. When they last parted, his mother's grief had been so intense Wynne wasn't able to penetrate it. Perhaps having Stephen and Lauren along would dispel some of Mrs. Reardon's pain.

Mrs. Reardon was sitting at a table in the officers' mess when Wynne and the children arrived for breakfast. She looked very elegant with her immaculately coifed white hair and impeccably styled green linen dress. The outfit complemented her hazel eyes and petite figure. Michael had often joked about the matching hazel eyes of his "two favorite girls."

Stephen and Lauren ran to her with a chorus of "Granny!"

"Hello, Dears. It's so good to see all of you." She patted Wynne's hand as Wynne kissed her cheek.

"You look lovely, Mother Reardon."

A white-coated waiter approached.

"Just coffee, please."

"Now, Dear, that's no breakfast," Mrs. Reardon chided. She had ordered orange juice and cereal.

"I know...I'm just not hungry."

"How about pancakes?" Wynne asked Stephen and Lauren. They both nodded in agreement.

"What will you do now, Wynne?" Mrs. Reardon asked.

"Do?" Wynne responded.

"I mean about staying in Florida. Will you keep your Gallery?"

"I plan to continue with the Gallery and keep the house," Wynne assured. "We've always considered it as home."

"That's wise," Mrs. Reardon said. "The first few months being a widow aren't a good time to make any major changes."

Wynne knew that only too well. Her own mother had been so devastated by Wynne's father's death, she couldn't make any decisions for almost a year. Then she'd made an abrupt decision to remarry -- a decision which turned out to be disastrous. Wynne and Michael had taken over everything for her. And Mrs. Reardon spoke from her own personal experience, too, although she had managed her life alone much better than Wynne's mother had.

A young lieutenant approached the table. "We're ready to leave for the White House at any time," he said quietly. "Captain Markham is waiting at the car."

"Thank you," Wynne said, taking a last sip of coffee. The children took a final bite of their pancakes, and the family all stood to go to the White House.

***

WYNNE CAUGHT A glimpse of the Mall after they circled the Capitol. Children frolicked around the Reflecting Pool and people strolled through the Mall area. *How happy those children are ... so unaware of the magnitude of a loss such as Stephen and Lauren are facing.*

The staff car quickly whisked them down Pennsylvania Avenue to the gates of the White House where a guard waved them through. The driver parked by the south door where a Marine guard stood smartly at attention. Chairs and a platform covered the south lawn. Flags flew briskly in the breeze around the podium.

Colonel Holmes met them at the portico. "The President would like to meet both of you before the ceremony," he said. They were ushered into the Blue Room where coffee and Danish were being served. President Richard Nixon and other dignitaries stood in a receiving line greeting recipients and family members. The two other recipients were in their full dress uniforms, resplendent with medals on their chest. Wynne's breath stopped and a small startled sound caught in her throat. The pain of Michael's absence astonished her -- *did it only worsen with time?* How strikingly handsome he was -- would have been, here in his uniform, if only this would have been such an exciting day for him.

Wynne, Stephen, Lauren, and Mrs. Reardon went through the receiving line. She met the Secretary of the Air Force Marshall Sterling and

Congressman Burroughs before being introduced to the President. Each shook her hand warmly, and told her how much the nation appreciated Michael's sacrifice for his country. She did not trust her voice, but silently nodded and shook each hand firmly. This was her last formal duty as a military wife -- she must do it well. Stephen's eyes widened as the President shook his hand.

"Your father was a very brave man, Son. Our country is proud of him."

"Thank you, Sir," Stephen whispered as he tried hard not to cry.

When the receiving line ended, the group was directed out to the south lawn. Wynne and the other recipients were seated on the platform while Mrs. Reardon joined Tom in the third row of the audience. The Marine Band struck up "Hail to the Chief" as a Marine guard escorted President Nixon to the platform. The audience stood until the piece was finished and then saluted the flag as strains of "The Star Spangled Banner" filled the air.

Secretary Sterling introduced the dignitaries on the platform, ending with the President. President Nixon then stood at the podium and called the two recipients by name. The first recipient walked to the podium and saluted. The

President returned the salute, read his citation, and placed the blue-ribboned Congressional Medal of Honor around the recipient's neck. He then awarded a Medal to the second recipient.

"...and Mrs. Wynne Reardon will accept the award posthumously for her husband, Major Michael Reardon," the President said. He read the citation for Major Michael J. Reardon's heroic actions, ending with "...for conspicuous gallantry and intrepidity at the risk of life, above and beyond the call of duty."

Wynne shook hands with President Nixon, and accepted the medal in its velvet box. A small fluttering in her chest spread through her limbs, and she was fearful the tremors would incapacitate her, that she might not be able to make it back to her chair. But she seemed to float effortless, away from the President, gripping the velvet box – her only reality in the vast emptiness of that moment. Then she saw a hand reaching out to steady her, and the tender sadness in the eyes of Tom Markham.

Chapter Seven

*September, 1973*

WYNNE FOUND HERSELF looking forward more each day to going to the Gallery. She denied, however, Jason's presence there had anything to do with her level of anticipation. It was, of course, her work that drew her there she reasoned.

His excellent pottery pieces continued to bring in the funds she needed for the Gallery. When she totaled the August receipts, the pottery sales led all the others.

Lauren seemed to have a special bond with him as he patiently showed her how to wheel throw pottery.

Wynne found him working diligently at the wheel as usual on Monday morning. "Man's work is never done," she said flippantly. "But you've surely made a difference for the Gallery. We're almost breaking even."

Jason laughed. "Is that a veiled suggestion to be more productive?" he asked.

"Not at all," Wynne said defensively. "Just a 'thank you' for helping to make the Gallery successful."

"You're welcome," he replied as he wiped the clay off his hands. "I think a picnic on the beach is in order..."

"Sounds good to me, too," Wynne replied. "Let's pick up some sandwiches at the Bay Deli. I'll tell Connie we're going..."

\*\*\*

WYNNE FELT THE refreshing salt air on her face as Jason's truck rumbled across the bridge to the island. Traffic was unusually sparse since it was a weekday.

The sea-scent filled her nostrils, and she felt exhilarated. She had forgotten how good it felt to relax. The familiar sight of the drifting dunes, stalwart sea oats bending in the breeze, and the relentless tides met her gaze as they stopped at the Gulf Islands National Seashore parking area.

Jason carried the picnic hamper, and she took the blanket as they walked down the beach to a small inlet area. She spread the blanket out on the sand as a sandpiper scurried for safe haven from the intruders.

They quickly ate the sandwiches brought from the Deli. Wynne felt total relaxation spread over her as the warm sun and sound of the sea surrounded her.

She looked at Jason's profile as he gazed at the Gulf. The square jaw and determined look seemed to be his hallmark. Just as Michael's gentleness seemed to be his.

"Jason, we need to discuss your position on the war," Wynne said abruptly. "It's a wedge between us that I'm having a hard time dealing with...we have to talk about it."

"Wynne, I don't want to talk about it. Besides...I don't think you're capable of understanding my position." Jason stood and brushed the sand off his jeans. He had a look unlike any Wynne had ever seen from him before. His face was drained of color and almost like a mask. "As far as I'm concerned, Vietnam is simply a name for loss," he said. He knelt down and drew the letters 'L - O - S - S' in the sand with his fingers, and then quickly brushed them away.

"But we fought there for ten years," Wynne countered. "That must count for something."

Jason shook his head. "We could have fought there for 100 years...the outcome would have been the same -- only the body count would have been different. The North Vietnamese were willing to pay whatever price for victory. They've been fighting for hundreds of years, and have outlasted everyone they've fought...They defeated us the same way."

"But we were trying to save a nation from communism." Wynne said.

"No, Wynne," Jason said, again with the tone as though he were humoring a child as he did during their first meeting. "We were trying for a stalemate -- not a victory. An impossible goal in a civil war. Besides, Wynne, this was a Vietnam "Era", not a war. That's our American euphemism for a war that was never declared."

"Perhaps if more people had supported it, we would not have lost the war," Wynne said.

"We did not lose the war. We simply chose not to win it. Besides, that war did not present a danger to the United States. We simply had an obsession to fight communism wherever we found it. And we fought it badly. Our bureaucrats limited our weapons, and curtailed our strategy. You cannot win a war with a policy of gradualism while the enemy throws everything they have at you. It was truly a political war. The political restrictions killed us."

Jason threw a shell into the surf, and watched it disappear into the frothing waves. His facial features relaxed for a moment.

Wynne looked at him angrily.

"But I can never forgive you for not doing your duty," she said. "How could you not serve your country?"

He looked toward the horizon where the blue waters of the Gulf of Mexico met the sky. He turned to Wynne.

"I did do my duty, Wynne. I served in Vietnam as a helicopter pilot. I made reconnaissance flights like those sent to find the wreckage of Michael's plane. We were pretty careful, and those reports are really accurate. That picture you saw in my desk was after my discharge

-- I was representing VVAW in that demonstration."

Wynne felt a twinge of guilt as she remembered rifling through Jason's desk. If she hadn't looked for that decorator's card, she might never have known about his stand on the war.

"VVAW?" she asked. "What is that?"

"Vietnam Veterans Against the War," Jason replied. "Who would know better than those of us who served there why America should be out of Vietnam? VVAW isn't all protest either. We work to improve veterans' conditions and job opportunities, and provide a support network for those who served. I don't need any lecture about duty."

Wynne didn't know what to say. Jason probably never would have told her about serving in Vietnam if she hadn't forced him to. She felt very foolish and wished she could take back her words.

"Jason, why didn't you tell me?" she asked.

"That's a closed chapter of my life, Wynne. It shouldn't make any difference now."

"No difference?" she asked. "It makes all the difference in the way I feel about you. My feelings for someone who protested and refused to serve in

Vietnam are quite different from those for one who served and then felt we should not be there. Why is that so hard to understand?"

"We just should not have been there," Jason said simply. "Guess we'd better get back," he added, putting things back into the picnic hamper and folding the blanket. "Man's work is never done, I believe is the battle cry."

Wynne smiled as they watched a sand crab burrow into his hole in the sand. "I wish I could follow him," she said softly.

***

THE NEXT DAY Jason stuck his head in her office door. "Miz Reardon, I need to have a word with you!" His brown eyes flashed as he entered her office waving a piece of paper.

She looked up from her desk. *Was Jason only teasing, or was he really angry?*

"What is it?" she asked with a bemused smile.

"This isn't funny," Jason said angrily as he thrust the paper at her. "You've scheduled me for an Art Show in Tallahassee on September 16th."

"And?" Wynne asked.

"And I have some commissioned pieces due that week," Jason said. "I can't go."

"You should have told me sooner," Wynne said with some annoyance. "You know how well your pottery sells at these shows. I thought you'd be pleased."

Jason's features softened. "Well, ordinarily I would be, but I made a commitment for some pieces for the Leonard Gallery in West Palm Beach."

"Very well, then," Wynne said. "I'll cancel our booth."

***

THERE SEEMED TO be some distance between her and Jason that Wynne had not noticed before their conversation on the beach, and encounter about the commissioned piece. It was a kind of aloofness she found hard to understand. *Perhaps telling me the truth has somehow made him feel more vulnerable.* He barely said a complete sentence to her the rest of the day. She reflected on Jason's stand on the war. *Since he had served in Vietnam, too, how had the war changed him and not Michael?*

The hum of the potter's wheel was the only sound in the Gallery as Wynne worked at her wall hanging. She frequently looked in Jason's direction, but he seldom raised his head from hovering over the potter's wheel.

Jean called later in the morning. "Wynne, dinner's at seven...hope you can join us...Stephen and Lauren, too."

Wynne was surprised at the unexpected invitation although she really shouldn't be. Jean often did things on the spur of the moment. That was one of her endearing qualities. She hesitated for a moment, and then said, "Sure, we'll be there...what can I bring?"

"Not a thing but you and the children," Jean assured. "Ray will be the chef for the Stearns' famous steaks."

Wynne laughed. "Sounds good."

Before she left the Gallery, Wynne stopped by Jason's work area, but he had already left. A neat array of pottery to be fired was by the kiln.

*** 

THE STEARNS WELCOMED Wynne and the children warmly when they arrived at their home. Wynne was surprised to find a fellow pilot of Michael and Ray's there, too. Jim Kaylor stood as she entered the room, and extended his hand.

"Wynne, how nice to see you again...it's been too long. Hickam I believe -- Thanksgiving?"

Wynne remembered all too well. *It was Hickam Field, and the Thanksgiving the squadron had dinner at the Reardons. Michael had smoked a turkey and...*The memories flooded back all too quickly. Wynne remembered Jim Kaylor was one of the most eligible bachelors in the squadron. He was a handsome man with blonde hair and mysterious gray eyes

"Yes, Jim, it was Hickam," Wynne said as she shook hands with him. "This is Stephen and Lauren."

"You look very much like your father," Jim said shaking Stephen's hand.

Wynne felt sudden tears as Stephen then stood up straight and said, "I know, Sir."

"Jon and Emily are having a picnic in the back yard," Jean said to Stephen and Lauren. The children scampered off to join them.

The dinner conversation was lively with Ray and Jim remembering many humorous anecdotes of their worldwide tours. Wynne noticed they were very careful not to mention Michael's name, although he had often been a part of their adventures. *Had Jean planned this dinner so she and Jim would be together or was it just a coincidence?* Jean couldn't help being a matchmaker.

Shortly after dinner, Wynne returned home relaxed and refreshed from her evening at the Stearns. There was something exhilarating about being part of the squadron again, a feeling she had missed during her widowhood.

The foursome for dinner reminded her of the many times she and Michael had shared meals with the Stearns. There was definitely a different feeling being a single person with a married couple and being part of another "couple." She really couldn't define the difference except she felt better there with Jim. And she wasn't once referred to as Michael's widow -- she was Wynne. *Could she really be just Wynne ever again?*

Somehow the idea of Jean's matchmaking attempt infuriated her. *How dare Jean presume to think she would be interested in Jim Kaylor -- or anyone else for that matter that Jean might coincidentally invite to dinner!*

She would just have to confront Jean about it. But it was a nice evening, she had to admit to herself. And for a fleeting moment the term, "widow", did not seem to be hovering about her. Stephen and Lauren seemed to enjoy the evening, too. *Perhaps it was because she was so relaxed.*

141

\*\*\*

WYNNE LOOKED UP from her workbench to see a blue uniform as Tom Markham arrived unannounced at the Gallery on Thursday morning.

"Hello, Wynne. How are you?"

"Fine, Tom. Are you glad to be stationed near Destin?"

Tom nodded and asked, "Would you go to dinner with me?"

Wynne shook her head. "No, I have a fiber piece to finish on deadline. I'm sorry."

Tom lowered his head. "I'm sorry, too, Wynne. Perhaps on my next trip."

Wynne nodded. "Yes, possibly...", knowing all along that she would never have a dinner date with Tom Markham unless the circumstances of Michael's death were more fully explained.

"I'll call you when I'm back in town," he said turning to leave.

"That will be fine," she replied, continuing to work on the fiber piece.

Wynne paused from her work, and thought about Jason's honesty about his stand on the war and Tom's possible actions -- and the deception she felt had surely taken place. The blue uniform did not make up for any deception. Tom's attentiveness in Washington had made her even more suspicious. *Was he attempting to remove his guilt over Michael's death by trying to be her strength now?*

*Would she ever know whether or not he caused Michael's death -- or at least if he could have saved his life?* The unanswered questions continued to haunt her.

***

TOM CALLED EARLY one morning later in the week. "Wynne, it's Tom Markham. I hope I didn't awaken you."

"Oh, no, Tom. I should be up by now anyway."

"I'm back in Washington and will be down there later today for a briefing. Would you have dinner with me?"

"Dinner...Oh, Tom, I don't know..."

"Please, Wynne. I need to talk with you."

"Well...all right, Tom. I can be ready at seven."

"That will be fine. I'll see you then."

Wynne put the telephone down and thought about Tom's invitation. She had vowed not to go out with him until the full story of Michael's death was revealed. *Perhaps she would learn something tonight.*

Before Wynne could get dressed, her mother telephoned. "Wynne, how are you?"

"I'm fine, Mother...and you?"

"Just a bit of bursitis in my shoulder. Otherwise I'm fine. Any more art events on your calendar?"

"Yes...there's a show at St. George Island on the 23rd. I do plan to attend."

"Now don't let anything interfere, Wynne. The military can do without you now."

"Yes, Mother," Wynne said, and quietly sighed.

"Tom Markham will be here tonight. I'm having dinner with him while Stephen and Lauren go to the movies with Ray and Jean."

"Ray's a good influence for Stephen," her mother said. "Stephen needs a father-figure."

Wynne's thought that mentioning the Stearns would offer her mother another track of conversation was short-lived.

"Oh, I'm so glad to hear that you're going to dinner with Tom Markham, Wynne. He's such a nice young man. Reminds me so much of Michael."

Wynne flinched. The last person in the world that would remind her of Michael would be Tom -- perhaps her mother wouldn't think that way if she only knew the truth. Then Wynne chided herself. *She didn't even know the truth. It was unfair to judge Tom until she did.*

"Yes, Mother, he is a nice man."

"Let me know about the Art Show, Dear. You know I want to hear."

"I will mother. Thanks for calling..."

Wynne sighed as she hung up the telephone. Her dear mother could no more stop her interference than she could stop breathing. It was suffocating at times. But Wynne loved her nevertheless -- her intentions were good anyway.

Before she could finish dressing, Jean called.

"Enjoyed dinner," Wynne said, trying to dress with one hand as she cradled the phone to her ear.

"I'm glad...you know you're family here," Jean said. She paused before asking, "And how did you like Jim?"

"Like?" Wynne asked. "What's not to like? He was a good friend of Michael's at Hickam."

Jean laughed. "I mean really like."

Wynne smiled. The dinner meeting was not a coincidence. In an effort to humor her friend, she said, "Okay I really like him. I have to run. Have a dinner engagement with Tom."

"Tom?" Jean asked knowingly.

Wynne explained, "I hope he will tell me more about Michael's mission."

Jean said softly, "Please give it up, Wynne."

"I can't," Wynne replied. "Talk to you later." She then hung up the telephone and finished dressing.

Ray and Jean stopped by for Stephen and Lauren just before Tom arrived, promptly at seven.

When Wynne opened the door, the image of Tom in his blue dress uniform with the array of ribbons of above his left lapel gave Wynne a start. Until she looked at his features, it was as though

Michael were standing there. Instead it was Tom's eyes she found riveted on her.

"Hello, Tom. Please come in. Let me get a wrap and I'm ready to go."

Wynne went to the hall closet, and got her favorite shawl, remembering that sea breezes even in September could be quite chilly.

Tom extended his hand. "Great seeing you. How have you been?"

"Managing quite well, thank you. The Gallery is a full time commitment you know."

Tom drove to the Officer's Beach Club that overlooked the Gulf of Mexico. Wynne inhaled deeply as they went over the bridge to the island as the sea scent filled her lungs. The feeling of total relaxation she had known earlier with Jason overcame her again.

She studied Tom's profile as they drove. Unlike Jason, she couldn't imagine him ever carrying a protest sign -- even as a Vietnam veteran. She thought he had the same commitment that Michael had -- although Tom's actions on the bombing mission were still suspect as far as she was concerned. *Could she possibly confront him on it? And what if he told her he was at fault. How could she deal with that?*

Tom parked outside the Club and opened the door for Wynne. "My", she remarked. "I've forgotten what chivalry was. It's been a while."

Tom laughed. "Just Air Force protocol, Ma'am," he said. "Remember, I'm an officer and a gentleman."

They dined on shrimp and salad while the surf lapped softly on the beach. Tom talked to Wynne about remembrances of Michael while they were stationed in Vietnam. Most of his conversation dwelt on humorous notes, but later his brow furrowed and he got a faraway look in his eyes.

He finally said, "We briefed for over an hour for that mission. We reviewed the route of flight, approach to the target, the weather and the enemy gun positions. Those tracers and airbursts that hit my plane came from nowhere...then I lost sight of Michael, and got disoriented as to where my targets were." He paused as his voice choked. "Wynne, I want you to know that I did everything humanly possible to find Michael in time. I really did..."

He reached across the table and took her hand in his. She drew back and clutched both hands in her lap.

*Why did he feel so compelled to tell her that? The official report had indicated that -- he had no need to continue his defense, unless that was just what it was -- a defense of his derelict actions.*

"I'm certain you did, Tom," Wynne said without conviction. "That's what the report said, too." She hesitated for a moment before asking, "But did you use proper judgment in your support of Michael's plane?"

Tom hung his head. Then he said quietly, "I'll always wonder, Wynne. By the time I sighted Michael again, he was trailing smoke from both engines." His voice became a whisper. "My plane was pretty shot up, too, so I just barely had time to see him eject, and follow his 'chute down to where he landed in the trees."

Wynne impulsively reached for Tom's hand and squeezed it gently.

Tom's eyes filled with tears.

They completed dinner in silence, and drove back to Wynne's home with only a few words. When Tom parked his car in her driveway, he said,

"Wynne, I asked the Casualty Assistance Officer if I could personally deliver Michael's things to you. I have his footlocker in my trunk. Do you think you're ready for it now?"

Wynne felt a catch in her chest and nodded. She had to face seeing his personal effects sometime. *It wouldn't get any easier.*

Tom got the footlocker out of his car trunk, and carried it to Wynne's living room. He placed it gently on the carpet, and handed her the key.

"Would you like for me to wait while you open it?"

She shook her head, her eyes transfixed on the stenciled letters MAJOR MICHAEL J REARDON.

Walking with him to the door, she said simply, "Thank you, Tom, but I need to do this alone."

"I know," he said, and kissed her gently on the forehead. He then turned and walked briskly out the door.

Wynne knelt down by the footlocker, and rubbed her hand over the stenciled letters of Michael's name. She thought about his life...class valedictorian, football captain...her first love...the all American boy that had stolen her heart on their first date. The small key fit readily into the lock that sprung open with a gentle turn, but she hesitated for a moment before raising the lid.

His leather flight jacket was folded neatly on one side of the locker. She took it out, held it at arm's length, and gently touched the name REARDON. How often he had held her close against that leather jacket! She pressed the soft leather to her face before putting the jacket aside, and taking out a bundle of letters. Thumbing through them, she saw they were all her letters -- dating back to the first one she had sent to Southeast Asia.

Among the personal grooming items, she found a snapshot of the two of them. They both had broad smiles as they hung precariously to a catamaran. Wynne remembered the occasion as one of their sailing adventures in Hawaii. Ray must have taken the picture. She really couldn't remember the circumstances.

She found a *New Testament Bible* tucked in a corner of the locker. Opening it she read the presentation page: To: *Michael James Reardon*, From: *Mother and Dad, November 29, 1954.*

*That was Michael's sixteenth birthday,* she realized. Noticing the ribbon marker, she turned the pages until she reached the marked section. Her eyes fell on 1 Corinthians 13. This Scripture on love had been one of his favorites. He had circled verse 13: "And now abides faith, hope, love, these three, but the greatest of these is love."

Dear Michael -- he truly had all three -- faith in his country; hope for the future; and indeed love. Her love for him would be forever. She put the *New Testament* back in the locker, and picked up the flight jacket again. After holding it to her for a moment, she put the jacket on and wept quietly. When Ray and Jean brought the children home from the movies, they found Wynne still wearing the jacket.

*** 

THE NEXT DAY Wynne worked hard to finish her tapestry. She wanted to be able to relax and enjoy an upcoming Art Show on St. George Island. She noticed Jason had not mentioned attending. *Would she be the only Gallery representative?* Before she could think more about it, he stopped at her work area. He looked steadily at her.

"Is St. George Island a go?" he asked.

She smiled at his directness. "Yes, indeed," she said. "Shall I send reservations for the Gallery?"

"It's just you and me," he replied. "Lorraine has another commitment. She asked me to take her paintings."

Wynne felt a sense of uncertainty about spending the weekend at the Art Show alone with Jason. She could no longer distance herself from him.

"All right," she said. "I'll reserve two rooms at the Island Hotel."

"This should be a good event for the Gallery," Jason said, then added, "we'll hope the Air Force honors your schedule this time."

Wynne winced. *How dare he intrude on her private world as Mrs. Michael Reardon! If she wanted to attend an Air Force function instead of an Art Show, that was certainly her decision to make. Jason's insensitivity was doing nothing to endear him to her. Why did she worry that there might be a problem with a personal relationship? Maintaining just a professional relationship would be enough of a challenge.*

She managed to calm down and call the Island Hotel for two room reservations. A very chatty lady took down the information, and tried to explain the entire Art Show agenda before Wynne abruptly cut her off.

"Yes, we'll arrive about seven p.m. on the 22nd. I want to guarantee the rooms for late arrival."

Wynne sighed as she hung up the telephone. Everything -- even the simple task of making room reservations -- seemed to be a chore. She wished she could just retreat into her safe cocoon of memories as Mrs. Michael Reardon and not face the world anymore. *Unfortunately, life did not offer that option.*

\*\*\*

WYNNE LEFT STEPHEN and Lauren with Jean. "Have a great time," Jean said. "We'll be fine."

Stephen and Lauren hugged their mother good-bye, and happily ran into the den to play board games with Jon and Emily.

Wynne then met Jason at the Gallery for the trip to St. George Island. He had already filled his truck with his pottery, and was struggling to load the potter's wheel and some display shelves he had made for the show.

"These demonstrations are a pain," he said with a wry smile. "I'm getting too old for this."

Wynne laughed and loaded the rest of her fiber pieces in her car trunk.

"I'll follow you," she said as she backed out of the parking lot.

***

ST. GEORGE ISLAND appeared on the horizon as Wynne followed Jason's truck across the bridge from East Point to the barrier island that reached out into the Gulf of Mexico.

Jason parked in front of the Island Hotel, and opened Wynne's car door as she parked beside his truck.

"My, smell that sea breeze," she said, breathing deeply and inhaling the salt-filled air.

"It is invigorating," Jason agreed as he took her by the arm.

The Island Hotel lobby was filled with other artists as Wynne and Jason checked into their rooms.

Wynne took a quick shower, and changed to her favorite green linen dress. She noticed how it accentuated her hazel eyes as she applied her makeup.

Jason gave a low whistle when she met him in the lobby. "My, I didn't realize I'd be escorting the belle of the ball," he said as Wynne blushed.

Wynne's reservations about Jason melted momentarily. *It was nice to have a man find her attractive again.*

They ate a candlelight dinner in a room overlooking the Gulf. Moonlight silvered the crest of the waves as the tide came in to the beach.

Wynne tried to keep the conversation focused on the Art Show.

"Think we'll have many commission opportunities?" she asked, looking around the room for prospective clients.

"Sure...this is a mecca for wealthy Alabamians. I'm sure we'll have plenty of requests," Jason assured.

Wynne laughed as an Alabama football fan walked by their table wearing a *Roll Tide* red sweatshirt.

"Certainly an entrepreneur," she quipped.

"Indeed," Jason agreed.

"How about a walk on the beach?" Jason asked as he paid the check.

Wynne agreed although in her heart she had serious reservations about being alone on a moonlight beach with Jason.

They walked down the cypress walkway to the edge of the water. The moonlight illuminated the beach with a soft glow. The night sounds of the surf murmured nearby.

Jason took her gently by the hand, and walked slowly along the sand as the surf lapped gently at their path. Wynne tried hard to forget other beach walks -- Waikiki especially.

Jason stopped at an overturned fishing boat and sat down. Taking her other hand, he pulled Wynne down by his side.

"It's a lovely night," she said, looking up at the stars. "So peaceful. If only our world could stay this way," she said wistfully.

"We have to work to keep it this way," Jason said softly. "If nothing else, Vietnam taught us lasting peace is never assured."

"But it takes a military commitment to assure it," Wynne countered.

Jason visibly stiffened. "Wynne, you have the Air Force rhetoric down to a fine science...peace does not always take military intervention. Diplomacy can also generate peace."

Wynne sighed. She was no match for Jason's rhetoric either. Her defense had always been Michael's statement, "We're making the world a better place to live." But his commitment -- and loss of life -- did not make the world a better place for her to live. *Could she possibly be leaning away from Michael's patriotic stand? Could a reasonable decision for non-involvement also be a patriotic stand?*

She looked up at the sky and sensed the tranquility of the moonlight spreading softly over the undulating waves. *Was there also a sense of tranquility entering her own life, too?* Wynne watched the gently breaking waves, and dared not seek an answer now.

Jason cleared his throat. "Would it be improper if the potter should kiss the boss?"

"Jason...I'm not ready..."

He lifted her chin and said softly, "I know it was not long ago that Michael was your life. And if you need distance, I will not press. But I'm sure there's a Wynne in there that could use someone who cares for her now." He kissed her gently on the cheek.

"Perhaps..." she said and put her head on his shoulder. They sat silently watching the receding surf in the moonlight as waves lapped at the shore. Wynne shivered as the wind increased, and Jason put his arm around her shoulder.

"How about a hot cup of coffee?" he asked. He glanced at his watch. "The coffee shop should still be open."

"Sounds good," Wynne said, snuggling into the warmth of his chest.

He pulled her to her feet. Wynne brushed the sand off her shirt.

They walked arm in arm back to the hotel, entered the near empty coffee shop, and sat in a booth near the back.

"Two coffees, please," Jason said as the waitress approached their table. They talked about the future of the Gallery as they lingered over the coffee. When Jason walked her back to her room door, he kissed her gently on the lips.

She nestled in his arms and said, "I never thought this might happen."

159

"I never doubted for a moment that it would," Jason said, kissing her again. "I can't go on like this...pretending we're just colleagues."

"But..." Wynne started to say.

Jason pressed his fingers gently over her lips.

"This isn't easy for me either, Wynne. It's hard trying to replace a memory."

*Could she really replace a memory?*

She had assumed she would be Mrs. Michael Reardon for the rest of her life. *Yet as Jason's arms drew her to him again, Michael seemed part of another world — a world that was now gone.*

## *Chapter Eight*

### *October, 1973*

AFTER THE TRIP to St. George Island, Wynne felt a mixture of emotions toward Jason. She plunged into her fiber work with increased intensity so she wouldn't have to think about their relationship.

Chaplain Turner's call awakened her from a deep sleep early on Friday morning. Glancing at the clock, she saw it was only 6:00 a.m. She reached for the telephone on the bedside table with alarm.

"Wynne..." Chaplain Turner said. "I apologize for calling you at this hour. There's been an accident...Tom Markham and Ray Stearns had to eject over the Gulf."

Wynne found herself suddenly very wide-awake. *Tom and Ray...in an accident?*

"Are they all right?" she asked.

"Yes," the Chaplain replied. "They are both very lucky. Our search and rescue team found them quickly. They've been taken to the hospital."

"I'll be there as soon as possible," she assured. She awakened the children, and they all dressed quickly. She explained what had happened to Ray and Tom as they drove to the base hospital.

\*\*\*

WYNNE FOUND JEAN Stearns in the family waiting room at Eglin Regional Hospital. She was huddled in a blanket, her eyes swollen from crying.

Wynne put her arms around her friend and hugged her tightly.

"Everything will be all right, Jean," she assured, echoing what Jean had promised earlier when Michael was MIA.

Jean started crying as Wynne continued to comfort her.

"Can I see him?" Wynne asked as Jean's sobbing subsided.

Jean nodded and led Wynne to Ray's room.

Ray was propped up in bed, his right arm encased in a cast. Jean kissed him on the cheek that brought a smile to his face.

"Hello, Wynne. It's good to see you."

"It's very good to see you, Ray. Hope the broken arm won't keep you out of the cockpit too long."

Ray laughed. "Considering the alternative, that's a minor problem."

Wynne smiled. She was relieved to see that Ray hadn't lost his sense of humor.

"Jean, would you and the children leave for a minute. I need to talk to Wynne." He patted his wife on the arm.

Jean nodded and gave him a hug.

After Jean, Stephen, and Lauren left the room, the smile left Ray's face. His eyes were very somber.

"Wynne, there's something you need to know before you see Tom..."

He paused and looked out of the window before continuing.

"Yes, Ray, what is it?" Wynne asked.

"I really hate to tell you this, but it will probably come out in an investigation if one is requested."

"Investigation?" Wynne asked. "Tom's?"

"I'm afraid so," Ray said. "He was doing some of his hot shot flying stunts, and we got a power loss from one of our engines. Then the other engine started to sputter. Tom was ready to eject right over Destin, and let the plane come down somewhere in town. It's only because I raised hell in the back seat, and called him every name in the book, that I got him to fly out over the Gulf before we bailed!"

"There's no telling how many people he would have killed if he let that plane go down in the middle of town!" Wynne said with alarm.

Ray was sputtering with rage again. "I almost punched him when they pulled us onto that rescue boat. You can bet I spilled my guts to anyone who listened to me about that idiot. That's why he's in trouble. He'll probably be grounded for an extended period if there's an investigation."

"But that's not what you want to tell me about, is it?" Wynne asked.

"No...it's Michael's mission. Facts have just come to light that show Tom had ignored the real mission of silencing the anti-aircraft, and flown off chasing a MIG. A MIG! Tom's old Weapon Systems Officer finally admitted it recently."

"Why would Tom do that?" Wynne asked.

"He always claimed he would be the first Ace in the squadron. Ya' can't be an Ace unless you shoot down enemy aircraft. So, he was off on a glory hunt, and not there to help Michael suppress those gun and missile sites like he was supposed to."

Wynne interrupted, "That's why Michael attacked so aggressively, isn't it?"

"I'm afraid so, Wynne. Michael knew the follow on bombers would be sitting ducks if he didn't silence those guns. So he pressed the attack, even with his WO dead in the back seat. That was a brave decision, and he had to know he might not survive. After his plane was hit that last time, he tried to gain altitude and fly back towards base, but he had to bail."

Anger overwhelmed Wynne. *If Tom's "stupid ego" had indeed been the cause of Michael's death, how could she possibly deal with that?*

She fought back tears. Ray reached out and took her by the hand. "I'm so sorry Wynne," he said. "So sorry..."

Wynne nodded. "I'm so glad you're going to be all right." She released her hand from Ray's grasp, and fled from the room. Jean was talking to Chaplain Turner in the hallway. Wynne tried to brush by them, but Jean caught her by the arm.

"Wynne...what's the matter?" she asked.

Chaplain Turner took her by the other arm, and led her to a chair.

"Ray told you, didn't he?" he asked gently.

Wynne nodded and blotted her eyes with a tissue. "Why?" she asked to no one in particular.

She was drawn into the same sense of helplessness and hopelessness she had felt when she first learned about Michael's death. And now to know that it was probably avoidable! *How can she be expected to deal with that?*

"I'm so sorry, Wynne," Chaplain Turner said. "Can you possibly find it in your heart to forgive Tom? He desperately needs that forgiveness now."

*Forgiveness?* The word reverberated through Wynne's thoughts. *How can you forgive someone who has taken your world away -- indeed your very existence?*

Numbness swept over Wynne's entire body. *The reality of what she had suspected was now confirmed: Michael might have been saved if not for the selfishness of his glory-seeking wingman! The nerve of Chaplain Turner asking her forgiveness!*

She shook her head and said, "No," as a flush of anger again reddened her cheeks. She took Stephen and Lauren by their hands, and quickly led them to the door. Their frightened expressions only compounded her anger. The terrible ache in her heart was made worse by their sadness. Their anguish, an anguish that obviously could have been avoided, devastated her.

***

AS SHE SAT at her desk at the Gallery, Wynne stared at Michael's picture. His smile reached out to her, and she traced the curve of his lips with her fingers.

"Oh, Michael," she said softly. "If only Tom had followed orders."

Her grief was now compounded by anger and guilt -- anger at Tom for letting it happen, and guilt that she couldn't forgive him for his actions.

Her thoughts were interrupted when Jason entered the office. She put down the photograph as he said, "Say, would a penny for your thoughts do?"

"I'm afraid not," she said wearily.

"Are you all right?" Jason asked with genuine concern, taking her by the hand.

"It's been a difficult morning," Wynne said. "I've been at the hospital with Ray Stearns."

"Yes, I read about the near collision in the morning paper. He's apparently a very lucky man - - Tom Markham, too."

"Yes, they are," Wynne said with an air of detachment. "Tom was Michael's wingman," she explained, looking again at the photograph.

"No wonder you're so concerned."

"I learned from Ray today Tom was the reason Michael was unable to make it back to the base..." Her voice trailed off, and she pressed the photograph to her chest.

Jason put his arms around her. The warmth of his body gave her a sense of comfort again.

He held her at arm's length, and put a hand under her chin. "Wynne, this hasn't changed anything...you still need to get on with your life.

Grieving over the reason for Michael's death won't bring him back."

"I know," she said softly," but Chaplain Turner wants me to forgive Tom...he's extremely depressed. I can't forgive this -- not ever."

Jason said quietly, "When you stand praying forgive, if you have ought against any..."

Wynne was surprised to hear Jason quote a Scripture verse from her favorite book of Matthew. It was something Michael would have said. "I know that's the Christian ideal," she said, "but how in my heart can I forgive someone who has killed the one I love?"

"Your not forgiving will not bring Michael back," Jason said simply. "And think of what it will do to Tom's life if you don't? We all have things to forgive."

He turned and quietly left the room.

Her first reaction was one of anger. *How dare Jason presume to tell her how to lead her life! If she wanted to hold Tom accountable for Michael's death, then that's her right.* She was angry at Jason for telling her what to do, and at herself for their romantic encounter at St. George Island.

"Oh, dear God, please help me!" she cried out. "Losing Michael is bad enough, but knowing someone he counted on caused his death is more than I can bear."   She clenched her fists in frustration and anger.

\*\*\*

WYNNE REFUSED TO talk with Chaplain Turner when he called the following week.  She felt there was nothing more he could say to change her mind regarding Tom.  So she was totally unprepared when he walked into her office on Friday.

Looking up from her work area, she was startled to see him standing by her.

"Wynne...I need to talk with you."

Wynne shook her head.

He reached out and gently touched her hand, "Wynne, don't let this destroy your future. Tom made a dreadful mistake...and he's paying for it now with a future filled with guilt.  Don't let your anger ruin your future and that of Stephen and Lauren, too."  Without another word, he turned and left the room.

Wynne looked up from her fiber piece, knowing in her heart Chaplain Turner was right. Her anger would only consume her.  Tom already had his guilt to live with -- probably for a lifetime. And she really didn't know all the facts. *Perhaps it would be best if she never did.*

She reached for a piece of stationery, and pensively looked out of the window at the tranquil surf before she wrote the letter.

*Dear Tom:*

*We have both been through significant losses, and need to find the strength to go on. As you no doubt know, I have held you responsible for Michael's death. I realize now that this is not fair to you. Michael made a decision to protect your plane, as any other pilot would have done. Please forgive me for my error in judgment as I forgive you. May Michael's favorite verse from the book of Matthew give us this peace. "When you stand praying forgive, if you have ought against any..."*

*Sincerely,*

*Wynne*

\*\*\*

WHEN WYNNE SORTED the morning mail on Monday, she found an official looking letter from the Department of Justice addressed to Jason. She took it over to the potter's wheel where he was working on a bowl.

"Thought you might be looking for this," she said with a smile.

"My future," he said holding the letter aloft. A smile crossed his face after he tore it open and read the contents.

"Good news?" Wynne asked.

"Very good! Our VVAW group will not be prosecuted for our demonstration at the Republican National Convention in Miami. All charges have been dropped...so you don't have a convicted felon on your staff." His brown eyes met her gaze with a warm, happy look.

"I'm glad for you," Wynne said, though she found it hard to accept any part of the protest movement. If the charges had been dropped, their right to protest had been accepted at the highest levels. *Did that make it right?* She didn't know.

"That's what America is all about," Jason said. "Freedom to be for or against something...our stand has been vindicated."

Wynne shook her head without saying anything. *She was expected to accept, or at least understand a stand against a war in which her husband had served gallantly and lost his life. And beyond this she was to forgive the one who had perhaps contributed to his death. How much more could possibly be expected of her?*

Wynne went back to her desk, and opened her own mail. The first letter was confirmation of her reservation for the Gallery to participate in the Art Show at Panama City Beach on November 16th. It would be good to get away, and just enjoy the outing.

A letter from Tyndall Air Force Base caught her eye. This was a base in nearby Panama City. To her knowledge, Michael had never had flights there -- his missions were all out of Eglin. She opened the letter and discovered it was from the Base Commander.

> *Dear Mrs. Reardon:*
>
> *We are having a Change of Command ceremony on Friday, 16 November, at 1400 hours. This is an invitation for you to be our special guest at this ceremony. Recognition of Major Reardon's gallant efforts in Southeast Asia will also be made at this time. We look forward to your presence at this ceremony.*

*Sincerely,*

*General John Grant, Commander*
*Tyndall Air Force Base*

Wynne sighed as she realized there was another schedule conflict. She would have to miss the Art Show at Panama City Beach. This would not be good for the Gallery because her presence was needed to make important contacts -- especially before the holiday season. Yet her presence for the ceremony at Tyndall was also necessary. She'd have to ask Jason to represent the Gallery again -- he would surely understand.

But her request fell on deaf ears. Jason's hands never paused on the wheel when she explained the Tyndall conflict. His eyes were somber as he looked at her.

"Wynne, this is your Gallery, and you need to be its representative. How long are you going to let the military hold you hostage?"

Wynne stiffened. *She was hardly a hostage! Attending military functions that honored Michael was a privilege -- not a duty.*

"I don't appreciate your comparison," she said hotly. "I'm still Mrs. Michael Reardon, and I will attend that ceremony."

"I thought there was a Wynne Reardon somewhere in there, too," Jason countered. "Or will it be Mrs. Michael Reardon for the rest of your life?"

Wynne wheeled and hurried away, too angry to reply. Perhaps Jason was right. *And what is wrong with that?* She looked at Michael's photograph.

A knock on her office door interrupted her thoughts.

"Come in..."

Jason waved a white cloth inside the slightly opened door.

She managed a smile at his actions.

"Temporary truce?" he asked.

She nodded.

"How about attending the Art Show at Panama City Beach, and driving over to Tyndall just for the ceremony?" he asked. "I'll cover your display while you're gone."

*Why didn't she think of that? Of course, she could do both.*

"That's a good idea," she agreed with a smile. "I can be Mrs. Michael Reardon and Wynne at the same time."

"That's a start," Jason said, patting her on the shoulder. His lingering look, however, gave her mixed feelings that were discomforting. She called and asked Jean if Stephen and Lauren could spend the weekend of the Panama City Art Show with the Stearns.

"Of course," Jean said. "We'd love to have them. Jon and Emily will be quite excited when I tell them Stephen and Lauren will be here for the weekend!"

## Chapter Nine

*November, 1973*

"IT IS AWE-INSPIRING," Jason said as he entered the Gallery's main room where Wynne was mounting her latest tapestry on the wall. "Here, let me help you."

He took one side of the piece while she nailed the hanger in place. He then hung the fiber work on the cedar wall, and stepped back to look at it. Rays of sunshine filtered through the louvered windows, and danced off the bright yellow and orange colors of yarn.

"It's as sunny as your disposition," he said with unusual schoolboy-like enthusiasm.

"What a nice compliment from my favorite critic," Wynne said, throwing a ball of yarn at him.

177

Jason deftly caught the yarn, and handed it back to her. His hand then held on to hers as he drew her to him and gently kissed her.

Wynne was caught so off-guard that she found herself responding to Jason's kiss and embrace before she realized what she was doing. She then pushed him gently away. "I'm sure you have some commission pieces to finish," she said.

"My unfinished business is here," he said gently kissing her again before he turned and strode to the door.

Wynne's heart and mind were racing as she watched Jason's figure go through the door. *What am I going to do about that?* She put away her supplies without having an answer.

*** 

WYNNE TRIED TO work on a fiber piece, but her thoughts kept returning to the circumstances of Michael's mission. She simply couldn't focus on her work, and put the frame down on the workbench

*How could she possibly attend the Change of Command ceremony at Tyndall Air Force Base where Michael would be honored? She would feel like a*

*hypocrite with her anger at Tom. Even Michael wouldn't understand her consuming anger at his wingman.*

She went into her office, and dialed General Grant's number. A brisk voice answered, "Commander's office."

"This is Wynne Reardon. I'm sorry, but I'll be unable to attend the ceremony on November 16th. Please advise General Grant."

"Yes, Ma'am," the duty officer replied crisply.

As Wynne hung up the telephone, she saw Jason standing in the doorway of her office.

"What's that all about?" he asked with a puzzled expression.

"I just can't go," Wynne said. "There's so much about Michael's mission I don't understand..." Her voice trailed off as she looked out of the open shutters of the windows at the breaking waves.

"What's to understand, Wynne?" Jason asked, taking her by the shoulder.

"I hold Tom responsible for Michael's death." Her hazel eyes flashed in anger as she spoke.

Jason sat her down gently in her desk chair, and leaned on one knee beside her. "Wynne, being out of his sector could have been a navigational error. After all, he was only human."

Wynne felt overwhelmed again by Jason's logical reasoning. He always seemed to have an answer, or an explanation for all of life's circumstances, but this time he couldn't change her feelings about not attending the ceremony.

"But I just can't attend the ceremony at Tyndall," she said. "Not now."

Jason stood up and looked down at her. "Wynne, attending that ceremony should not depend on your anger at Tom. It's the husband you loved who's being honored. The fact is that Michael still died defending his country whether Tom's plane was in the right sector or not!"

Wynne met Jason's gaze. "I'll go to the Art Show," she said firmly, "but not the Change of Command ceremony."

Jason shook his head and left the office.

Wynne walked out to the deck of the Gallery where she always found peace. She stood there taking in the spectacular sunset. The sun's orange ball slowly slipped beneath the water on the western horizon. A purplish hue then engulfed the beach.

Jason returned and walked out of the deck to join her.

"We OK?" he asked.

She nodded and felt an arm encircle her waist, and caught the familiar scent of Jason's after-shave lotion.

"It's always beautiful isn't it?" he asked, looking at the sunset, and drawing her closer to him.

"Yes," she murmured, nestling in the crook of his arm.

They stood together silently as the last fading rays of sunlight radiated over the water.

Jason kissed her lightly on the cheek.

Wynne pulled away and sat down on the wicker swing.

He sat down beside her and took her hand in his. "Let's don't argue, Wynne...especially about a Change of Command ceremony."

She simply nodded and put her head on his shoulder.

***

THE FOLLOWING WEEK was Thanksgiving. This November seemed more like 11 years rather than 11 endless months since January. This was one year she would like to awaken and find the entire holiday season had passed. She would find it hard to match the spirit of a grateful nation. It would be the first Thanksgiving in many years that the news had not been filled with body counts from Vietnam.

*What was there for her to be thankful for anyway this year?* Michael's photograph on the mantel seemed to look back at her. Pride and sadness filled her chest as she looked at the array of combat ribbons and medals on his uniform.

"We're making the world a better place to live," he had assured her when he left that last time. But her world was so empty now. Even the children's presence couldn't fill the void of Michael's absence.

*What did life have to offer now for a 35-year-old military widow whose life had revolved solely around her children and her husband's career? Her existence was only in his reflection. She indeed had been Mrs. Michael Reardon, wife and mother, for thirteen years and had wanted no other identity. Everything reminded her of him -- a remembered word -- the refrain of a song -- an American flag. His memory was inescapable. Would this aching ever end?*

The previous months had been a nightmare for Wynne. She managed each day in a state of shock. But now the acceptance of his death was quite another matter. She felt she was expected by the military community to be the stoic military widow, and cheerful mother of two bewildered and lonely children. *How could she possibly manage that?*

Wynne fingered the mandala on her worktable. The off-the-loom fiber piece had been started for a wall hanging in their den. She hadn't had the heart or the desire to finish it. He had liked her design very much. It reminded him of Waikiki, he said. *Maybe if she finished it now...*

Michael had encouraged her to continue her work in fiber art. It wasn't easy transporting all of the looms, fibers, and books during their numerous moves, but he had always insisted.

"We'll never be stationed anywhere long enough for you to have a real studio," he said after they were first married, but you can always use the living room if you like."

The weaving interest had gotten her through many lonely nights. There was always another commissioned piece, an art show, or a friend needing assistance with a project. *But how could she possibly fill a lifetime now with weaving projects?*

\*\*\*

PANAMA CITY BEACH was busy with activity as other artists set up their booths when Wynne and

Jason arrived for the Art Show. They checked in at the reception area, and were directed to their respective adjacent booths.

Jason helped her mount her fiber art on the lattice framework of the booth.

The brilliant colors of the yarns, as usual, brightened the entire area. Jason then unloaded, and quickly displayed his pottery. Wynne noticed he had brisk sales immediately.

The afternoon went by quickly. Wynne sold several major fiber pieces, and took orders for three more. As she talked to a restaurant owner about a tapestry seascape he wanted to order, she heard the unforgettable sound of F-4s overhead. She looked up to see the planes from the Change of Command ceremony at Tyndall as they completed their fly-over of the base. As she saw the precise formation fly overhead, an enormous wave of guilt swept over her.

The buyer appeared alarmed at her stricken look. "Mrs. Reardon, are you all right?" he asked with concern etched in his features. As the jets disappeared into the clouds, she nodded and returned her attention to the plans for the commissioned piece.

Wynne and the buyer came to an agreement on the content and price of the fiber piece.

184

"My wife would especially like to have sea shells and driftwood incorporated into it," he said.

"Certainly," Wynne said with a smile as she handed him a copy of the contract.

Jason stopped by her booth after the Art Show ended. "It's been a good day for me," he said. "How about you?"

"Fine," she replied. "I have an excellent commissioned piece to do."

"Let me help you put away your pieces," Jason said. "Then we can have some dinner."

"I'd like to change first," Wynne said.

Jason laughed. "But then my jeans won't be appropriate."

"Well then, you change, too," she said with a laugh. "By the way, my small loom needs some repair. Did you bring your tools?"

Jason nodded and said, "Of course."

***

WYNNE MET JASON in the dining room of the Sandpiper Lodge where they were staying. The hostess seated them by a window where they could see the moonlight illuminating the surf. Jason ordered seafood gumbo for both of them. "It's still a national treasure," he said with a mischievous smile.

Although they talked mostly about the Art Show, Wynne noticed that Jason was looking at her in a quite different way. There was a sensitivity about him that she hadn't noticed before. After they finished a delicious seafood dinner, Jason asked, "Do you still need for me to fix your small loom? I have my tools in the room."

"Wynne said, "Yes, I use it to show customers how I do the off-the-loom pieces. I'll need it tomorrow."

Jason and Wynne stopped by her room after dinner to get the tapestry loom.

As she turned to hand the loom to him, he kissed her with an intensity of passion she did not expect.

She then managed to murmur, "Jason, I don't think..."

"That's right," he said. "Don't think...just feel what's right for us."

He turned and left her room quickly.

Wynne stood quietly in the middle of her room after Jason left. *How could she feel so at peace? She had almost forgotten how delightful it felt to be embraced, and held in such a loving way.*

\*\*\*

ON THE WAY back to the Gallery after the Art Show, Wynne was unusually silent. Jason looked over at her with a smile.

"Guess a penny wouldn't do it," he said.

Wynne was totally absorbed in her thoughts and didn't reply.

Jason put a hand on her arm and said, "Wynne, what's the matter?"

She looked at him with regret in her eyes. "You were right. I should have gone to that ceremony."

Jason looked pensive for a moment before he spoke. "I thought you were perhaps thinking about us. Wynne, going to ceremonies should be a choice, not a duty."

"But I failed to honor Michael's memory...In several ways..." She couldn't continue.

Jason pulled over to the side of the road, and took her hands in his.

"Wynne -- it's been 11 months since Michael was declared killed in action. You've done nothing, but sustain his memory all this time. It's not a crime to miss one ceremony. It was only a Change of Command ceremony -- there will be others. Others over which you'll have no conflict."

Wynne nodded reluctantly. She had to admit Jason was right. *But why was it so hard to let go?*

Jason leaned over and his lips brushed her forehead. "You have a life, too, Wynne. Enjoy it!"

***

WYNNE'S SPIRITS BRIGHTENED somewhat the following week as she worked diligently on the commissioned pieces, and was pleased with their development. As she paused in her work, she remembered the feel of Jason's warm embraces. It was a feeling she had almost forgotten. She smiled and experimented with new bolder colors of yarn.

In Tuesday's mail delivery, she found an invitation to submit a piece for national judging. She thought about the seascape she was designing for the restaurant. There would be time to enter it into the contest before it was due to be delivered to the buyer. She worked on it with renewed interest.

After sketching the design for the wall hanging, Wynne decided to go to the beach to get seashells and driftwood to incorporate into the completed piece. She had some apprehension about inviting Jason to go with her since the beach was usually deserted this time of year. Yet it would be a good chance to be with him, and enjoy his company away from the Gallery.

He seemed absorbed in his work on a large bowl. She watched his strong hands deftly molding the spinning clay. Those were the same strong hands that had held her in his arms. She waited for him to complete the piece. He looked up at her with a smile.

"Interested in a trip to the beach?" she asked. "I need to sketch a design, and find some shells and driftwood for the tapestry I'm doing for the contest. And I also need a bodyguard," she added with a smile.

"Sure," he said, wiping the clay off his hands, and covering the piece with a damp cloth. "Give me a minute...one bodyguard will be ready to go."

Wynne laughed and went into her office. She realized when she sat down at her desk it was the first time she hadn't looked at Michael's picture when she first entered the room. That had been a ritual for 11 months. Jason was right. She had lived in Michael's memory all this time. *Was she possibly beginning to let go?*

Jason stuck his head in the door and interrupted her thoughts.

"Ready?" he asked.

"Sure," she said, and grabbed her tote bag without glancing at the photograph.

\*\*\*

THE BEACH WAS deserted except for the shorebirds when Jason and Wynne arrived. They spread a blanket on a sand dune amid sea oats whispering in the wind. Their graceful stems bent with each passing breeze.

Wynne assembled her sketching materials on the blanket, and gazed at the beach scene. Jason stretched out on the blanket, propping himself on an elbow, and watched her begin to work.

"How can tide lines provide a design?" he asked with interest as she sketched. His look stirred passionate feelings, and she tried to avoid his gaze.

"No mystery. Forms left by dried salt, debris, and sand provide a design that's impossible to create from imagination."

"If you say so," Jason said with a smile. He lay on his back, and watched the cloud formations as she worked.

Wynne sketched the design, thinking about materials she would use in weaving the piece. But it was impossible to focus totally on her work, as she was acutely aware of Jason's presence next to her.

To the side of her sketch, she penciled in ideas for yarns, textures, and colors. "Try seaweed," she noted with a burst of enthusiasm. "Use jute for warp," she added to the pad as a reminder to purchase some heavier rope to use for textural contrast.

Sketch and ideas finished, Wynne tossed some sand on Jason's feet. "Let's go," she urged as she scanned the area for shells and driftwood she could add to he finished work as a final touch of nature.

She pulled him to his feet. Their laughter echoed along the beach as they playfully kicked sand and surf at each other. Despite the many times Wynne was exasperated with Jason, he could still make her laugh. And it was a good feeling – one she hadn't experienced enough in almost a year. The tide lapped softly on the shore while they walked. The idyllic scene was disturbed only by the occasional cries of shorebirds as they dove into the water for fish.

Wynne and Jason continued to walk hand in hand along the beach, each silently absorbed in thought. Wynne could feel the strength of Jason's strong hand as he firmly held hers. She unconsciously compared him to Michael – the strong hand holding hers; the handsome profile; the muscular, lean body...*How many similar strolls on the beach had there been – walks on Waikiki and the Gulf Coast?*

Chiding herself for making such a comparison, she clasped Jason's hand more firmly and increased her stride. She loved these kinds of mornings on the beach, and dug her toes into the warm sand while they walked. She leaned over and picked up several shells that lay in her path. The surf provided a perfect sand dollar. It was still a natural color, unbleached, possibly still alive. She tossed it carefully into the water.

"Look!" Jason said, pointing seaward.

A large sailboat appeared on the horizon, its sails spread to the wind. They stopped and watched the vessel as it passed. The craft turned across the wind toward open water with its rail well under, sailing fast. A broad river of foam came from the side of the boat. The rail quickly emerged from the water as the boat was turned off the wind.

"How free!" Wynne whispered as they watched the boat.

"Life should be that free," Jason agreed, squeezing her hand gently.

Waves thundered to the beach as the wind increased. The tide was rising and whitecaps foamed when the wind picked up in intensity. The sky suddenly became gray with threatening thunderheads.

Wynne and Jason ran down the beach to get her sketching supplies as raindrops spattered them. She grabbed her tote bag while he threw the blanket around them as they ran for shelter. Breathless and soaking wet, they found a thatch-covered picnic area, which gave them some protection from the rain. Wynne laughed and brushed at the sand that has fallen off the blanket onto her arm.

"We must make some fashion statement," she said, her auburn hair plastered against her cheeks.

Jason brushed the sand from his jeans, and gave a wry smile.

They huddled on the picnic bench, and watched the angry sea. The sailboat came around in the direction of the moorings. Whitecaps pounded against her side. The person at the helm began sailing toward the dock. As the mainsail was loosened, the speed of the vessel slowed. Heaving ground swell rocked the boat with a vicious attack, but the vessel stayed upright.

Wynne was practically hypnotized at the beauty and drama before her. *Did the person at the helm of the boat share the excitement she felt? She sensed an oneness with this person. He, too, must sense the need for the freedom she longed for, freedom to be Wynne without the mooring of a memory she had so desperately clung to for 11 months...a memory that needed to be put to rest.*

Sails were etched against the darkening sky momentarily. Wynne hardly realized that she was getting wet as the rain blew into the shelter. She had one last glance at the sailboat when the helmsman started the engine and furled the sails. The sailboat was then deftly brought to the mooring under engine power. The boat smoothly slipped to the dock despite the intensity of the waves.

Wynne shivered as the cold rain continued to blow into the shelter. Jason put his arms around her, and drew her close to him. She had almost forgotten the warmth and sense of security such an embrace provided until he entered her life. She started to move away, but it felt so good to be in his arms again. She relaxed and nestled against him. Looking up at his handsome face, she saw the intensity in his brown eyes.

He looked down at her for a tender moment before his lips found hers, searching for her mutual need of him. Her response was at first tentative and uncertain, but then her lips parted with an unconscious invitation. She wanted to pull away from his embrace, but could not and found herself responding to his kiss. When their eyes finally met, she murmured, "Jason, I'm not sure..."

He put his fingers gently over her mouth and shook his head. Neither of them expressed their feelings of the moment. She tasted the salt spray on her lips as she nestled closer to him. As the storm raged around them, the circle of his strong arms protected her. His body against hers filled her with sudden longing.

The thunderstorm stopped as suddenly as it began. Wynne felt relieved they could now leave the shelter, yet she felt a sense of radiance she had not known for months. Her warm feelings were reflected in the gold and orange hues dancing across the crest of the waves as the sun burst through the clouds.

\*\*\*

AT THE GALLERY *the next week, Wynne questioned how she could continue to work with Jason.* He had caught her in unguarded, vulnerable moments when she desperately needed someone. She had been trying to deal with her anger at Tom. Jason had been there with his warmth and security. *Was that all she could see in him – a security blanket?* She had to admit honestly her attraction to Jason was more. She must resolve to keep only a professional relationship with him in the future. Her memories of Michael and sense of guilt over this new relationship would allow nothing more. How could she let Jason know the new ground rules without having her rejection impact their professional relationship? *What a mess she had made of her life.*

Wynne tried to keep her contacts with Jason at the Gallery to a minimum. She refrained from any personal comments, and kept the conversation to topics relative to the Gallery. His attitude toward her remained the same; his good-natured disposition and friendliness didn't change despite her aloofness. *Had he even noticed?*

She finished the commissioned piece for the restaurant on Friday, and packaged it for mailing to the national contest. A Blue Ribbon would add some more credits for the Gallery, and give it national prestige.

\*\*\*

IT HAD BEEN two weeks since the beach outing when Jason stopped by her office. He shut the door and pulled a chair up to her desk.

"We need to have a disarmament talk," he said, his brown eyes flashing.

"I don't know what you mean," Wynne responded defensively.

His brows furrowed, and his brown eyes sharpened.

"Wynne, I'm not Michael – I can never be Michael – and I do not want to take Michael's place. Can we establish that at the outset of this discussion?"

"I don't think I want to have this discussion," she said, looking out of the window at the Gulf.

"Please humor me – I do want to have it," Jason said. "I can't help it that I find you attractive, and I will not be treated like a delinquent child because of my feelings."

Wynne looked surprised and said, "But I didn't mean to..."

"But you did," he said firmly, his voice rough with emotion, and walked out of the office.

## Chapter Ten

*December, 1973*

WYNNE AGAIN FOUND solace in her work at the Gallery after Jason's confrontation. *A delinquent child, indeed,* she thought angrily! *Perhaps he should have said petulant child. That's the way he's acting. And he's right, he's not Michael, and he certainly cannot take Michael's place. Whatever gave him the idea that he could?*

Her angry thoughts continued to race until she settled into the rhythm of weaving. It had a calming effect as she worked on another sunburst design, and her thoughts were again on her work. The fiber piece quickly began to take shape.

Connie came into her work area and said, "Your mother is on the telephone."

Wynne nodded and went into her office.

199

"Hello, Mother."

"Wynne, Dear. How are you...getting ready for another Art Show I hope?"

"I'm fine. I'll probably go to one soon," Wynne said, not having a firm date or place in mind, but not ready for another lecture on "the Gallery is now your life."

"And how is that nice young man, Tom? I hope you're seeing some of him – he's so much like Michael..."

Wynne stiffened and thought, *No, Mother. Not at all like Michael.* She didn't feel like telling her mother about the circumstances of Tom's actions during Michael's flight so she said simply, "He doesn't get back to Eglin often."

"That's too bad, Dear, but perhaps you'll meet someone soon."

Wynne winced. *Why did there have to be someone? She had someone in memory – she had her children and her work* – and she thought wryly – *and mother's the one who said, "Your life is now your Gallery." How could "someone" be a part of that? Unless, of course, the "someone" was Jason, an idea completely out of the question.*

"It's good to hear from you, Mother. I'm really fine and will call soon..."

"I suppose you're busy, Dear. I'll look forward to your call."

Wynne hung up the telephone with a sigh. Relationships were not easy, she decided, reflecting on Jason's reaction and her mother's intrusion in her life. *Why couldn't people just honor her feelings, and let her lead her life her own way?* And even Jean's "match-making" was an intrusion she could do without. She knew that she didn't need another pilot in her life. Even in peacetime she could not bear to endure the wait through dangerous China Sea assignments again. Jean had almost lost Ray over the Gulf of Mexico – not the South China Sea!

Wynne worked diligently until noontime, and glanced over to Jason's area often, but he was never there. She had promised Connie and Lorraine a luncheon meeting so they could talk about some plans for the Gallery. She put away her work, and went to the Gallery reception area where she found Connie and Lorraine waiting for her.

"Sorry I'm late," she said. "I didn't notice the time. Where is Jason? I thought he would be with us. We need his input, too, in these plans."

Connie looked uncomfortable as she said, "He had a luncheon appointment and left earlier."

"I see," Wynne said. "Well let's go to the Bayou Tea Room. I can get with him later about our ideas. I'm sure he'll want to be included in our plans."

"Sounds good to me," Lorraine said, closing the massive wooden door, and hanging the OUT TO LUNCH sign on it.

The hostess led them to a table by the window overlooking the picturesque bayou. They ordered quickly and were enjoying the seafood luncheon when Wynne saw Jason enter the room. He was engrossed in conversation with a tall, fashionably dressed brunette. Wynne felt her stomach tighten, and tried to look away. But it was too late. Jason brought his companion over to the table. "Well, this must be the Executive Board meeting," he said with a smile.

"Not quite that formal," Wynne said stiffly.

"I'm about to forget my manners," Jason said, turning to his companion. "Diana, let me introduce you to my colleagues at Shoreline Gallery – Wynne Reardon, Connie West, and Lorraine Marshall. This is Diana Moore, Berkeley's renowned potter."

The introduction hardly relieved Wynne's tension, and she was angry with herself. *Renowned potter indeed! Why should it matter who Jason took to lunch? Or the fact that she was an exceptionally attractive woman?*

Wynne managed a civil, "It's nice to meet you. Perhaps you can stop by the Gallery while you're in town."

The woman nodded politely, and held on possessively to Jason's arm as they left for their table.

Wynne's lunch was ruined. She could hardly focus on the food and caught herself watching the animated conversation Jason appeared to be having with his friend. *Had she flown from Berkeley to be with Jason? Who was she anyway?* Connie and Lorraine did not appear to pick up on Wynne's distress and kept up a continual chatter about plans for the Gallery. Wynne finally excused herself and said, "I'll see you back at the Gallery."

"Without a slice of Death by Chocolate?" Connie asked with her youthful exuberance.

Wynne smiled wryly, "You'll have to eat a piece for me," as she left the table.

Wynne removed the OUT TO LUNCH sign from the wooden door at the Gallery, and opened the heavy door. The large cavernous interior of the Gallery seemed unusually oppressive in spite of the bright wall hangings covering the walls. She flicked on the light switch, and breathed a sigh of relief as the lights brightened the room.

As she walked toward her office, she stopped at Jason's area. Her hand ran over a bowl he had just fired. The smooth glaze felt like glass. She thought about the strong hands that had made it, and how he seemed to caress the clay into shape. Those same strong hands that had taken her into his arms. *Had those hands held Diana in the same way?*

Wynne had to admit that she was jealous of this woman, who had suddenly intruded into her life. She didn't know anything about Jason's past relationships. Maybe she was just a pottery colleague, and not a romantic interest. But the way she had clung to Jason's arm at the tearoom certainly gave support to the romantic interest possibility.

"Why can't Jason just be there for me when I need him?" Wynne whispered aloud. She then recognized the selfishness of her thoughts.

\*\*\*

JASON WAS THERE for her in the ensuing months in a professional sense. He continued to produce outstanding pieces of pottery, thus ensuring the Gallery's financial success. His handyman efforts were also unflagging – the Gallery was never before in such good shape, both physically and financially.

Because of the Gallery's successful status, Wynne was invited to present a seminar for the Small Business Administration. David Chambers, Director of the SBA, talked with her at length about her speech, and how much it would mean to other aspiring small business owners.

She was delighted with the opportunity to share her knowledge of managing a small business. As she prepared her presentation, she thought about how proud Michael would be of her – their dream was finally a reality. And it was a dream that was now providing her future without him.

***

AFTER A BRIEF introduction by the SBA Director, Wynne looked over the audience with a lump in her throat. Although she had prepared well for the presentation, she felt nervous. Yet when she began her talk, she relaxed and enjoyed sharing her success with the Gallery. Each time she glanced in Jason's direction, he gave her a broad smile of encouragement. She wished that she could give proper credit to him for the Gallery's success, but she knew that it would embarrass him if she did.

"...and market research is a key to having a successful enterprise," she concluded. "We couldn't have found a more receptive area than Destin for our Gallery. Our original market research indicated this before we even bought the property."

The director of the SBA stood as the audience applauded her speech. "I'm sure Wynne will be happy to entertain any questions," he encouraged.

Wynne nodded and a distinguished gray-haired man on the last row raised his hand.

"Yes?" Wynne said with a smile.

"What will you do with the Gallery when the state closes the highway for a State Park?" he asked.

Wynne responded, "I'm sorry, Sir, but that is not currently under consideration. Such a situation would be devastating, of course, to any business."

The man nodded his head. "Yes, I know, but there are rumors that the road will indeed be closed, and the area made into a State Park."

The SBA Director David Chambers responded. "Uh, hum, we've heard that rumor, and it has no basis in fact. Are there any other questions?"

Wynne answered several questions about financing and inventory before the meeting was concluded. Afterwards, she approached Mr. Chambers and asked, "That question about the road closing took me completely off guard. You don't think there is any basis to that, do you?"

Mr. Chambers rubbed his forehead with his handkerchief. "I'm afraid some conservation interests are pushing for the road closing. Our office had hoped that it wouldn't reach the public until we could get our facts ready. But obviously some word is out. Can you imagine what it will do to this community if that road is closed? It's a lifeline for the area businesses."

Wynne's heart sank. *If the road were closed, it would be the end of the Gallery. A call to Commissioner Mark Williams would certainly be the first thing on her list of things to do tomorrow.*

As they drove back to Wynne's home after the SBA meeting, she was unusually quiet.

The speech went very well," Jason said, patting her on the hand. "I'll let you manage my business anytime."

Wynne turned to see his handsome profile in the moonlight, and her heart quickened as he held her hand.

"I'm really concerned about the road closing rumor," she said. "I guess talking to Mark Williams tomorrow will be the first step to clarifying this."

"I wouldn't be too concerned," Jason assured. "It's inconceivable that any special interest group – conservation or not – would have the power to close a major road." He squeezed her hand gently. Wynne put her head on his shoulder, and hoped he was right.

Wynne called the Commissioner's office early the next morning. "This is Wynne Reardon at Shoreline Gallery. I'd like to speak to Commissioner Mark Williams," she said, tapping a pencil nervously on the telephone.

"Wynne, how nice to hear from you! How's everything at the Gallery? Helen is still thrilled with her wall hanging. It's really a masterpiece."

"I'm fine, Mark. Just concerned about a rumor that I heard last night. What about the possibility that the highway could be closed to make this area a State Park?"

There was a pause on the other end of the line. Wynne could feel her heart beating as she waited for his reply.

The Commissioner finally answered, "Wynne, I don't quite know what to say. Yes, the possibility does exist. The Emerald Coast Conservation League has an incredibly strong lobby in Tallahassee. They are pushing for the area from just west of your Gallery to the Walton County line to be declared a State Park. It will take some strong opposition from area businesses to nip this in the bud."

"What can we do at this point?" Wynne asked. "My Gallery is very important to me. I'm ready to do whatever is necessary."

"Petitions will help," Mark advised. "And letters to your Representative. Lots of letters. A State Park looks mighty good on a politician's record in this era of conservation minded people."

"I'll certainly do what I can," Wynne said. "And thank you for the information."

"You're welcome, Wynne. I'll be glad to help in any way that I can. Our community's economic welfare is very important to me."

*And your re-election is dependent on it*, Wynne thought wryly as she hung up the telephone.

Wynne went to Jason's work area after her conversation with the Commissioner.

"It's not all rumor," she said with a frown, and told him what Mark Williams had said. "That would mean closing the highway," she concluded.

"Well, we'll just see about that," Jason said, wiping the clay off his hands with a determined look.

\*\*\*

WYNNE AND JASON contacted all of the area businesses in the geographic location that might be designated as the State Park. Most had not heard the rumor, or if they had heard it, they had given little credence to it.

Jason tirelessly circulated petitions throughout the county and presented them to the Commissioner's office with the required 2,000 signatures opposing the closing. His dedication to the task surprised Wynne. Although considering his efforts as a Vietnam Veteran Against the war, she realized she should not have been surprised at his level of involvement when there was a just cause at hand.

Wynne thought back on the effort she and Michael had been involved in when the federal government had decided to make a national seashore in Navarre. They had both worked tirelessly to assure the stretch of land would be preserved as a wilderness area. Developers would not be allowed to build high-rise apartment buildings and obliterate the shoreline. *But how was this different? The developers were businessmen, too, with financial interests at stake.*

She mentioned her concern to Jason.

He laughed out loud at her comments.

"Good grief, Wynne. You're surely not equating Shoreline Gallery with a high-rise development on the beach. There's no comparison! Shoreline Gallery contributes to the conservation concept by providing beautiful objects that remind us of our heritage – pottery, weavings, and artwork. Get off this guilt trip and get in touch with reality. How can you fight for a cause you really don't believe in?"

"But I do believe in saving the Gallery," she responded defensively. "Yet, it's a selfish belief – it's my financial future."

"What you do here helps the aesthetic beauty of the area, Wynne, and yes, the economy if you

211

wish to look at it that way. That road closing would be an economic disaster for this entire county."

Wynne nodded. Jason was always the voice of reason, and she should know better than to try to out talk him on any issue.

***

THE WEEKS FLEW by as Wynne prepared the Gallery for the first Christmas Open House. She worked tirelessly preparing festive exhibits, and addressing invitations to the December 16th affair. *It was as though if she could stay busy enough, she could block out Michael's memory, the specter of the possible road closing, and Jason's presence -- a presence that bothered her very much whenever she allowed herself to think about it.*

She caught herself on occasion watching him work at the pottery wheel. That handsome face, those finely chiseled features captivated her while he was totally absorbed in his work. She chided herself for watching him, and especially for wondering what he might be thinking. He had worked so hard to help keep the highway open. *What were his motives? She hoped that it was more than just his personal interest as a potter at the Gallery.*

\*\*\*

THE CHRISTMAS OPEN House on Sunday was an enormous success. Wynne looked radiant in a red silk dress she had made for the occasion. Jason even reluctantly wore a suit and tie for the event.

"Mom, this is really cool," Stephen said, looking quite adult in his blue suit.

Wynne nodded and took him by the elbow. "There are some people that I want you to meet." She steered him to a couple engaged in animated conversation in front of a fiber piece.

"It's one of Wynne's best pieces," the woman said. Her companion, an Air Force Colonel, nodded in agreement.

"Charlotte...Greg, I'd like for you to meet my son, Stephen." She turned to Stephen and said, "These are the Morrisons. We were stationed at Hickam Air Force Base with them when you were two years old."

Colonel Morrison extended his hand. "Good to meet you, Son. I'd know you anywhere. You're the image of your father."

"That's quite a compliment, Sir," Stephen replied extending his hand to the former officer.

213

"Well, he was a fine man. You should be very proud of him."

"Lauren, please join us," Wynne called to her daughter, who was helping to pour punch at a nearby table. "And this is my daughter, Lauren," she said, and went through the introduction to the Morrisons again.

Commissioner Williams approached the group, and extended his hand in greeting to Wynne. "I would like to personally thank the person who has saved our highway, and perhaps our community."

"You mean..." Wynne said with excitement.

"Yes, your petitions have done the trick. They will designate this area as a State Park, but will keep the road open for business, too. It's really a miracle. I thought the Emerald Coast Conservation League lobby was too powerful to be deterred. But Mrs. Reardon, you have done it!" He kissed her on the cheek.

"You have Jason Garrison to thank for most of the effort," Wynne said, her eyes bright with excitement. "It was his battle, too."

"Well, whoever is responsible, the community owes him or her a big vote of thanks. I see you two are quite a team," Commissioner Williams said with a broad smile.

"Yes, I think we are," Wynne replied, surprising even herself with the statement.

***

SHE FELT AWKWARD when she and Jason met at the punch bowl -- her conversations with him had been so limited of late, except for discussions about the possible road closing, she hardly knew where to begin.

Jason sensed her uncomfortable feelings, and a smile creased his face. "A hello, how are you would be fine," he said. "Hello, how are you?"

Wynne blushed, her face matching the color of her dress.

"I'm fine. Thanks for all of your efforts."

"At your service, Madam," Jason said, clicking his heels together.

"Oh, Jason," Wynne said with exasperation. "You know what I mean. Your unique pottery has made the Gallery financially successful, and now you have single-handedly stopped the road closing."

Jason nodded and taking Wynne by the elbow guided her gently to the deck overlooking the Gulf of Mexico. He took her glass of punch from her, and placed it on the table. He then took her hands in his -- his brown eyes had a seriousness she had not seen before. "Wynne, I'm glad the Gallery's successful, and that I've been able to contribute to that -- but that's not the main reason I've stayed."

Wynne tried to pull away from him, but he continued to hold her hands firmly.

"I cannot express my feelings to Mrs. Michael Reardon. I only hoped that in time you would become Wynne again, and that I could be a part of your life. Will that time ever come?"

Wynne was not shivering on a beach now, cold and defenseless as Jason drew her into his arms. She saw him as the attractive, exciting man he was; one for whom she could no longer deny her feelings. It was the Wynne he sought who wordlessly responded to his kiss.

"Why me, Jason? It's not like I made myself emotionally available."

"You were so fragile that I was drawn to you. But in doing so, you revealed your strength. You defended Michael, not because he was the hero he was, but because your love for him was unassailable. What man could not want that for himself?"

Wynne examined Jason wistfully, but with a newfound respect. She simply nodded, as Jason continued.

"I love you and I'm sure that Wynne agrees, but maybe not Mrs. Reardon. Will you think about becoming Mrs. Jason Garrison?" he asked. "Perhaps later when your issues with the loss of Michael are resolved..."

"Maybe...I love you too..." Wynne murmured. *But when would resolution of the loss of Michael ever happen?*

The relentless waves pounded the shore beyond the deck as the eternal sea continued its landward journey. The moonlight shimmering on the breaking waves seemed to be an affirmation of the bright hope for their future. *There was the successful Gallery and Jason in her life -- but ultimately, now perhaps she was becoming Wynne.*

In an effort to shift the conversation, she said, "I've been giving something considerable thought." She paused as Jason looked expectantly at her.

"I would like for you to become a partner in Shoreline Gallery. What do you think?"

"I would be honored," he said, "And perhaps this will lead to the partnership I really want to have."

\*\*\*

*Early 1980s*

SHORELINE GALLERY THRIVED in the early 1980s with Jason's artistic work and partnership. Their collaboration as artists ensured its success. Jason had finally refrained from discussing marriage. In their last encounter on the subject, he reminded Wynne that he had dated a lot of women in the interim, but no one he had met was a "Wynne". Even that acknowledgement did not sway her determination to remain a widow, Mrs. Michael J. Reardon. He speculated whether or not she would ever give him a chance.

As time passed it became harder for him to accept her reticence. Frustration at times flirted with anger. So when he had an opportunity to establish his own gallery, he left to launch Surfside Pottery Studio in Pensacola. He and Wynne stayed in touch, but he did not have to face a daily encounter assuming his love for her was not going to be returned. He remained a business partner in

Shoreline Gallery, and continued to supply the Gallery with pottery as the years went by. Both Shoreline Gallery and Surfside Pottery Studio flourished.

## *Chapter Eleven*

*February, 1986*

WYNNE PUT THE finishing touches to the fiber piece she was completing for an Art Show in Cedar Key. She held the piece aloft and admired the sunburst design with its vibrant colors of orange and yellow. The piece mirrored the coastal sunsets that she and Michael had watched so often and so long ago. She sighed. *Dear God, will I ever see another sunset that I won't think of Michael?*

She refused to allow that old sadness to take away her pleasure in the mandala -- very possibly a Blue Ribbon design as though such recognition really mattered to her.

Actually the satisfaction of her creative efforts as a fiber artist meant more to her than any awards, but the reality was that awards were good publicity. She glanced at the awards on the wall that she and her fellow artists had received through the years she had owned Shoreline Gallery. They were good for business. It hardly seemed possible she would soon celebrate the fourteenth anniversary of the opening of the beachfront Gallery.

With the fiber piece completed, she gathered up her things to leave for the day. She stopped the pottery workroom to see if Jason had delivered some more pieces. She smiled when she saw his museum quality pieces were lined neatly on shelves he had so carefully crafted many years ago.

As she left the Gallery, she locked the massive wooden door, and then paused on the deck to watch the waves surge toward her as the waning sunlight filtered through the swirling waters. The incoming tide made deep inroads on the shore as the relentless waves continued landward. She never tired of it: the rise and ebb of the tides that shaped and reshaped the shoreline.

She drove the familiar beach road home with the car windows down, listening to the breaking waves. Their rhythm slowed her breathing, and gave her a sense of tranquility. When she pulled into her driveway, she paused to get the mail from the mailbox. A postmark from Alaska caught her eye as she flipped through the letters for any correspondence from friends. *Could Greg and Charlotte possibly still be there? How many years had it*

221

*been since Michael and she were stationed with the Morrisons in Hawaii? More than she could remember.*

She unlocked the front door to her home, a cedar-sided contemporary in a stand of pine trees. It was her refuge in the sheltering pines that seemed to capture every cool breeze that stirred. Their needles spread out in a canopy providing structure and framing for the house.

She threw her keys on the credenza in the hallway, and took the letter from Alaska from the stack of mail. When she tore open the envelope, a photograph fluttered to her feet. She looked down at it, then to the framed photograph on the sideboard. She felt a tightening inside herself, and her hands started to shake. She looked back to the picture on the floor, then bent down and stretched out her hand to touch it.

"Hi, Mom."

"What? Oh." She turned a startled face to her daughter, who was home from college for a visit, standing in the doorway. Lauren had the same wonderful smile she saw in the framed photograph. Wynne's lips quivered.

"What is it, Mom?" Lauren saw the picture on the floor, and dropped to her knees beside her mother. "What is it?" she asked again.

Wynne Reardon reached out, and touched the face of the man in the photograph. "Someone sent me a picture of your father."

"Of Dad?" Lauren's eyes widened as her mother picked up the photograph. "But who...?"

"It's from Greg Morrison. He was stationed with your father in Hawaii."

Wynne looked more closely at the photograph. The man had a beard and appeared to be in his mid-fifties. He was very thin, almost gaunt in his appearance. But there was no mistaking the eyes and the set of the jaw. It was Michael! She quickly read the letter from Greg.

> *Dear Wynne,*
>
> *I don't want to get your hopes up, but one of my friends just came back from Southeast Asia with some photographs of unidentified Caucasians who could possibly be American MIAs still alive over there. The friend was looking for his brother, missing somewhere near the North Vietnam border. This picture looked so familiar. Could it possibly be Michael? My friend gave me the enclosed card of the Operation Recovery Agency that searches for MIAs. Perhaps they can be of some help. Charlotte sends her love.*
>
> *Fondly,*
> *Greg*

Wynne's heart raced. She studied the photo again. *Could it possibly be Michael? Had he really been alive these 14 years?...Where?...How?...*

Her thoughts were a whirlwind of emotions as she fought to catch her breath. *Who should she call?*

Immediately, she thought of Chaplain Turner, the kind man who had brought her the news about Michael 14 years ago. The Chaplain had been there for them through their loss. He would want to help them discover the truth now. The Chaplain was a Colonel, and had retired in the Destin Area.

"We'll call Chaplain Turner," she told Lauren

"And how about Jason?" Lauren asked softly, interjecting cold reality into the statement.

*Jason, dear Jason. How would the man who had helped make her Gallery successful, and asked her to marry him possibly feel if Michael were found to be alive...?* Wynne couldn't pursue that thought now. She just had to find out more about Michael. "Jason will come if we need him," was all that she said.

Lauren's blue eyes sparkled. "Mom, maybe you've always been right that Dad is alive even though the State Department was so sure he didn't survive."

"What do they know?" her mother replied. "They never retrieved his body. It's certainly possible this is a recent picture."

Lauren's eyes glistened with tears again as her mother dialed the Chaplain's number. *She dared not get her hopes up again. Perhaps she should call Stephen.* But she knew what her brother would say. His angry statement echoed in her thoughts: "Why didn't Dad go to Canada instead of Vietnam, then we'd have a father and not just a second-hand memory!"

Lauren shivered at the remembrance of Stephen's outburst, and how deeply it had hurt their mother. She decided to wait to call Stephen. Stephen would no doubt still be at his office at Delcom in Washington writing some new super computer code.

Wynne dialed Chaplain Turner's number first and then Jason's. His well-modulated "hello" immediately reassured her.

Lauren continued to study the photograph. Her thoughts were interrupted by the sound of her mother's excited voice talking to the Chaplain.

"It's Wynne...could you come over please? I need to talk with you as soon as possible." She looked at Lauren. "Chaplain Turner is coming right over. He'll know what to do."

Wynne studied the photograph as she waited for Chaplain Turner and Jason. The person in the picture was sitting on a wooden bench. The bearded figure wore jeans and a plaid shirt. His blonde hair was slightly graying at the temples, and the blue eyes had that look that could penetrate into one's soul. That was one look she could never forget. She strained to see the date of the newspaper that he held. It was dated December 10, 1984!

Lauren stared at the photograph, too. She was only nine years old when her father's fighter jet was shot down over North Vietnam. The features of the stranger in the photograph were only vaguely familiar to her.

The ringing doorbell interrupted their study. Wynne hurried to answer it and welcomed Chaplain Turner warmly.

"How nice to see you again. We're so glad you came back here to retire."

"Wynne, what is it? You sounded urgent. Are you all right?" he asked and put a comforting arm around her shoulder. The Chaplain's eyes had that familiar look of fatherly concern she had been able to rely on these past years. His white hair gave him an appearance of distinction while his slightly stooping shoulders were the only sign that he had yielded to his age.

Her eyes brightened as she handed him the photograph. "It's Michael," she said simply.

"Michael?" He looked intently at the picture. "Wynne, are you sure?"

She nodded and as her hazel eyes danced with excitement said, "I'm positive."

The ringing doorbell interrupted.

"I asked Jason to come, too," Wynne said.

Jason embraced Wynne, and then tilted her face upward, tracing a tear with his thumb. "Wynne, what's the matter...it isn't about Stephen is it?" he asked, his brow etched in concern. Seeing the Chaplain, he extended his hand. "Nice to see you again, Sir." He turned to Lauren, studying her face for some clue to the sadness.

"There's news about Michael," Wynne said. "This is a recent photograph of him." She held the photograph out to Jason.

Chaplain Turner said, "Wynne's news is very...tentative."

"How recent is this photograph?" Jason asked, peering at it closely.

"Look at the date on the newspaper! It was only two years ago...it's got to be Michael," Wynne insisted.

"Where did this photograph originate?" Jason asked.

"One of Greg Morrison's friends just brought a number of photographs back from Southeast Asia of MIAs and POWs who are thought to be still alive," Wynne said. Her hazel eyes were steady and unwavering. "He also sent me a business card of an agency which investigates these cases."

The Chaplain shook his head. "Now Wynne, you know there has been a lot of fraud connected with the MIA and POW situation...people taking money to find traces of a loved one. This could be a fabrication...a cruel hoax."

"Yes," Jason agreed. "You must be very careful, Wynne. It's highly unlikely that Michael could still be alive."

She took the photograph from the Chaplain. "That's Michael," she insisted. "I'd know those eyes anywhere...even after 14 years."

"Well," the Chaplain said, "we should have someone in the State Department investigate this further. May I take this with me?"

"I'm sorry, I can't bear to part with it," Wynne said as she took the picture from him, and clutched it even more tightly. "I'll have a copy made and drop it by your office. When will you know something?"

"It may take several weeks. I'll call as soon as I hear anything," Chaplain Turner promised. He patted her on the hand. "Don't get your hopes up, Wynne. If it's Michael, it would indeed be a miracle."

Lauren slipped her arm around her mother's shoulder as Wynne bit back a denial. Wynne was too excited to believe that it was not Michael.

"In the meantime, I'll give your name to the National League of Families for more information on this agency. They have been strongly committed to the POW/MIA issue." Chaplain Turner moved to the door. "Perhaps they can verify the credentials of this search group."

After Chaplain Turner left, Jason drew Wynne down beside him on the sofa.

"Let's reason this out the way we discuss business dilemmas."

"This isn't business, Jason. This is my husband's life."

Jason was silent a moment, but continued. "Wynne, the I.D's in Vietnam were pretty accurate. If his crewman saw his lifeless body hanging in a parachute, then you must accept the fact that Michael is dead."  His voice softened as he said, "Wynne, I truly want Michael to be alive, too.  I really mean that...I'm sorry to seem so cruel, but you must look at the reality of this situation."

"The first official designation was killed in action, body not recovered," she said.  "I've always felt in my heart that there might be a possibility that he really did survive. That he was just unconscious..."

Jason restrained his anger at Wynne's stubbornness not to accept the facts.

"Wynne, these official reports are rarely wrong. Please consider that."

She only shook her head in response.

Jason caught his breath sharply.

"Wynne, I've supported you, your search for Michael, and the Gallery for 14 years. I've dated other women in the intervening time to forget you...and I can't.  What will it take for you to let Michael go and accept my feelings for you?"

He turned abruptly and left the room.

Wynne wiped tears from her cheeks, and joined Lauren in the kitchen.

"Mom, shouldn't we call Stephen?" Lauren asked from the kitchen.

"Of course. Will you do it?"

Lauren nodded and dialed her brother's number at Delcom. "Stephen, Mom has some news about Dad..." Lauren then explained about the photograph, and listened quietly for several moments. She brought the telephone to her mother. "He wants to talk with you."

Wynne took the receiver. "It's exciting news, Stephen. Don't you agree?"

"Now, Mom. Please don't get your hopes up. This sounds really bizarre."

"Please don't say that until the Pentagon can investigate the situation."

"All right, Mom," Stephen said, and she heard him sigh. "I'll get in touch with the Defense Intelligence Agency at the Pentagon," he promised.

***

The week crept by as Wynne anxiously waited for word. She tried to keep busy. Even Stephen's doubts didn't minimize her hopes. The house was especially quiet after Lauren returned to college.

Wynne walked the stretch of beach that had been Michael's favorite. The ever-changing seashore had always provided solace when she sought it there. As she strolled along the crystal white sand, she watched a sandpiper scurrying along the beach searching for food. The little bird's frantic actions seemed to be a mirror of humanity in its search for sustenance.

She tried working longer hours at the Gallery to help pass the time. The sunburst mandala she had just completed brightened the entire room, and buoyed up her spirits. How exciting it would be to have Michael come home to learn that she had made a success of the Gallery! *How could they regain the 14 years they had lost from their lives? It didn't matter. He would be home, and everything would be perfect again.*

Even her dreams were filled with thoughts of Michael. She saw him running on the beach -- his blonde hair tousled with the sun's gold. She felt his strong arms around her and his tender kisses. "You're so perfect to come home to," he would often say on his return from some faraway assignment.

Wynne tried to remember Michael's caresses. She longed for his tender touch. Every part of her being reached out to him. She had lost all sense of time and space when she was in his arms. *How could she ever hope to have that with Jason?*

Lauren's question, "And how about Jason?", brought Wynne back to the present. It was Jason who had been there, and given her comfort for all of these past years. *But she couldn't think about that now...*

\*\*\*

Wynne's evening hours were often filled with calls from Stephen and Lauren. They had supported her fully after the loss of Michael even though each had a different view about their father's fate. Lauren shared her mother's hope that her father could be still alive, while Stephen felt the facts made it impossible to deny that he was dead.

"Mom, how are you doing?" Stephen asked. His voice always made Wynne's heart skip a beat because it sounded so much like Michael's. "Any new developments?"

"No, I'm waiting to hear from Chaplain Turner."

Stephen paused before replying. "Mom, I've already talked to Colonel Hale at the Defense Intelligence Agency. He said there are several documented cases of this type of fraud..."

"No, Stephen, I don't want to hear that. Let's hear from Chaplain Turner before we rush to any conclusions."

Stephen paused again, then said. "All right, Mom. I'll call back tomorrow."

Lauren called, too. "Mom, are you okay? Has Chaplain Turner called?"

"Yes, I'm fine, and no, he hasn't called," she said. "I'm very anxious to get word, of course, but I know these things take time."

"Mom, I talked to my professor in International Relations today about the picture of Dad -- I mean the picture that looks like Dad. Dr. Avery remembered a reported sighting of 30 or so American pilots in Central North Vietnam, back in 1980 working on a road gang. He said that a spy-satellite had confirmed that a prison camp had been built near that area. Dad really could still be alive."

Wynne's heart quickened ... of course it was within the realm of possibility. "I believe that, too, Lauren, more now than ever. The CIA's Bangkok Station received similar reports at the end of the war. Americans were reportedly seen among the other prisoners working on road and irrigation projects. It's certainly encouraging news." *Even as she spoke, she sensed the dark despair and suffering that would be Michael's lot if he were alive under such conditions.*

Jason listened patiently when she talked about the possibility that Michael could still be alive, but offered little encouragement.

***

On Saturday morning, Wynne was startled by a knock on her front door. A gray-haired woman with friendly blue eyes and a warm smile greeted her.

"Mrs. Reardon?"

Wynne nodded.

"I'm Janet Morgan of the National League of Families. Chaplain Turner contacted me and asked me to talk with you."

Wynne's hopes soared.

"Yes, please come in."

She ushered her visitor to the den where they sat by the fireplace. Wynne handed her visitor the framed photograph of Michael, together with the snapshot of the bearded likeness of him.

"What a handsome officer," Mrs. Morgan said, handing the framed photograph back to Wynne, and studying the other one briefly.

"Yes, he is very handsome," Wynne agreed, emphasizing the present tense. She searched Mrs. Morgan's kind face for signs of encouragement, but found only sympathy and understanding.

"I don't want you to get your hopes up over the photograph. We have been investigating several of these recovery groups for some time. One organization has raised more than six million dollars, reportedly to find missing men in Southeast Asia. In one case, they provided a recent color photograph that purported to be a missing pilot. The picture was fraudulent. It caused the man's family untold emotional grief -- not to mention a substantial financial loss. Your picture could have originated with such an agency."

"But that is a picture of Michael," Wynne insisted.

"It well may be a photograph of Major Reardon," Janet Morgan agreed. "It could have been taken before 1972, and altered to make him look older. I'm not saying that is actually what has happened, but I don't want you to get your hopes up until the Air Force can do further investigation."

Wynne shook her head. *The date on the newspaper was real. The likeness was remarkable.*

The representative continued, "The MIA issue received the highest national priority under the Reagan administration. President Reagan expanded the POW/MIA section of the Defense Intelligence Agency in an effort to obtain information. He also had a team in Southeast Asia searching for information about the whereabouts of your husband and many MIAs."

"But his body was never recovered," Wynne said. "Didn't they search the site where his plane went down, and not find a trace of him? Isn't it possible that he could still be alive?"

Mrs. Morgan sighed. "It is highly unlikely. The sites that were searched were as uncertain as the recollections of the Vietnamese, and the surviving flight crews. The POW/MIA issue has been coordinated through the POW/MIA Interagency Group that included the Defense Department, the White House National Security Council staff, the State Department, the Joint Chiefs of Staff, the Defense Intelligence Agency, and our organization. We have investigated every lead...exhausted every shred of evidence every time an MIA issue was brought to us."

With a stroke of a bureaucratic pen, Michael had been declared dead even though his body was never recovered. Wynne put her head in her hands. Janet Morgan reached out and patted her on the shoulder. "I'm so sorry, Wynne. I know this is doubly hard after so many years."

"You're wrong!" Wynne blurted out angrily. "That is a photograph of Michael...he is alive. Why won't you believe that?"

Janet Morgan stood to leave. "My Dear, the League of Families hopes for miracles, too, but we deal with reality. We know how painful this is and how cruel these hoaxes can be. If anyone has information about your husband, ask him or her to turn it over to the Defense Intelligence Agency. Don't pay opportunists to do what your government will do for you."

After her visitor had left, Wynne tried to think of some way that the government military organizations could have overlooked some bit of information. Her thoughts were interrupted by a telephone call from Chaplain Turner.

"Wynne, I sent the photograph to Colonel Jim Hale at the Defense Intelligence Agency, and I'm afraid there is bad news. Although the photograph is unusually clear and convincing, they believe that this is an altered document. Perhaps a photograph of Michael when he was younger that has been doctored. I'm so sorry Wynne...I know that you had your hopes up."

Wynne's stomach tightened as Chaplain Turner confirmed what Janet Morgan had said. *Why won't these people accept the facts?* But all she could say was, "Thank you for trying..."

She called Stephen and Lauren with the Chaplain's report.

"I'm so sorry, Mom," Lauren said, her voice catching.

"Please, Mom," Stephen encouraged, "Accept the DIA's report on Dad."

***

After the Chaplain returned the copy of the photograph the next week, Wynne took the letter she had been saving from Michael and put it in the chest of drawers along with the copy of the photograph. The eyes seem to say, "Yes, it is really me." She was haunted by it.

She tried to return to a semblance of normalcy in her life after Janet Morgan's visit and the call from the Chaplain. Yet she found it hard to let go a nagging feeling that something may have been overlooked. Intellectually she knew the facts proved Michael was dead -- but emotionally, until his remains were found, there was always a glimmer of hope that he could possibly be alive. She could not let that die. She picked up the telephone, called Colonel Hale's office at the Pentagon, and made an appointment to see him the following Tuesday.

Later that evening she told Jason about her plans after he had stopped by to deliver some more pottery.

"Let me go with you," he offered. "I could ask some questions you might not think of."

'No," Wynne replied. "I have to do this alone." She paused and added, "Although I'm sure Stephen will insist on being with me."

"Wynne, I want to help you," Jason said, taking her by the hand.

She shook her head.

"No?" he asked, "Because of me, Wynne?"

She shook her head again.

"Because of what we've shared instead of you and Michael?"

240

She whispered, "No."

"Wynne, what we've shared...what we have is real. This guilt you have will destroy you if you let it." Jason let go of her hand and added, "Well...all right. Please call me after you talk with Colonel Hale."

"I will," she said softly and kissed him on the cheek.

She started to call Stephen and Lauren, and then thought better of it. Stephen would no doubt think that making an appointment to see Colonel Hale was absurd. After all, it was his office that had officially declared Michael dead. Lauren would have her hopes raised again. Wynne decided to wait until it was time for her to make the trip to tell them.

***

Jason stopped by just as Wynne had turned on the TV to listen to the evening news. Peter Jennings of ABC News appeared on the screen, and reviewed the presidential candidates' activities of the day. *At least they aren't debating wartime decisions like Nixon and Johnson faced in Vietnam*, she thought as she half-heartedly listened to the report.

When she heard the statement, "American POWs", her eyes were then riveted on the screen where Russian president Boris Yeltsin was speaking, the interpreter's voice dubbed over the Russian words.

"...and there were U.S. POWs from the Vietnam War that were transferred to Soviet Labor Camps..."

Wynne caught her breath. *Michael...could he be...?*

Yeltsin continued, "Our archives have confirmed some Americans were kept in labor camps or mental hospitals in the territory of the former U.S.S.R, and some may still be alive."

The words "may still be alive" reverberated through Wynne's thoughts.

Yeltsin concluded his speech with the caution, "There are people in our country that will do everything within their power to keep us from providing answers to the fate of these American servicemen."

"Have you heard about this before?" she asked Jason, her eyes blurring with tears.

"Yes, Wynne...I'm not surprised. I'd heard the term "Moscow Bound" POWs before, but there was never any proof."

"But why would the Russians want American servicemen?" Wynne asked.

"It's simple...Moscow backed North Vietnam with supplies and advisors. The Soviet Military needed the expertise of the pilots who were captured. Their technical knowledge would be quite valuable to the Russian Military weapons technology."

"What specific knowledge did Michael have that they would want?"

"He was an experienced pilot of an advanced combat aircraft, and he had information about avionics, AF weapons and current aerial combat tactics."

"Surely Americans would not cooperate willingly," Wynne said, her voice catching in her throat. "I know Michael would never reveal any of our secret technology."

"Those gulags and mental hospitals could have changed the strongest resistance," Jason said softly. "No, I'm sure they did not do it willingly."

She shuddered. As much as she wanted Michael to be alive, she could not wish upon him 14 years in a Russian gulag or mental hospital. *Hope and reality seemed to be at war in her head.*

Jason pulled her to him, and she did not resist the circle of his arms. "Are you all right?" he asked.

"I'm fine," Wynne said, keeping her voice steady. "When I see Colonel Hale, I'll ask what information the DIA has on Operation Recovery."

***

On the way to the Gallery, she turned her car radio to the public broadcasting news station. She heard a chilling statement by the Chairman investigating the POW/MIA issue that government officials had intentionally provided misleading and erroneous information about when and where some servicemen were lost.

Wynne thought about her letter from General Arnold that told her Michael had been killed in action on the North Vietnam border. *Was this one of these misleading and erroneous reports? But why? Perhaps Jason would have an idea because he was a Vietnam veteran, too.*

When she arrived at the Gallery, she was surprised to find him in the pottery work room.

"Just delivering some pieces," he explained as he unloaded a crate of finished pottery. He stopped and put an arm around her shoulder.

"And how are you now?" he asked, his brown eyes reflecting genuine concern.

"Confused," she answered. "Why would our government lie about where or when our servicemen were lost?" She told him what she had heard on the radio. "Why would they declare Michael dead when that might not be true?"

"American pilots, like Michael, flew missions over North Vietnam in great secrecy. These were mostly night missions, very high risk. I flew a helicopter called The Quiet One out of a guerrilla base that took commandos into North Vietnam. The chopper's sound signature was so low it could not be heard by the enemy until we were within about 900 feet. The commandos were able to put voice activated tape on the North Vietnam telephone lines southeast of Vinh."

"Did this end the war sooner?" Wynne asked.

"That's how we intercepted critical intelligence data that Henry Kissinger used in the Paris-Peace talks. This information gave us valuable insights into Hanoi's mind-set during the final days of the war. All of this action in North Vietnam was highly classified then. Michael may well have been a part of this mission. He may have been flying cover for the commandos. We'll probably never know for sure what his real mission was...or whether they know what really happened to him. We do know they lied about a lot of things."

Jason took his belligerent stance, feet apart, arms crossed over his chest. He had been active in Vietnam Veterans Against the War, a cause they had argued about it in the beginning. "He was reportedly shot down on the Vietnam border. Because of our covert operations in North Vietnam, his crash site could have been falsified for security reasons. But this is just speculation, Wynne." He took her hand. "You're trembling," he said tenderly. "This can only bring you more pain..."

Wynne just shook her head, and turned to go to her office. She kept the office radio tuned to the news station as she half-heartedly looked through the orders for some commissioned pieces. She heard an advisory that in light of the startling news that some Americans captured in Vietnam might have been held in Russia, there would be an investigation of these charges.

She couldn't wait to get to Washington. She would ask Colonel Hale what he expected this investigation to find. *Some of our missing pilots?* She was so stirred by the thought, she shivered. *But what if the investigation did not turn up any facts about the MIAs or POWs?*

She picked up the Operation Recovery Agency's business card from her desk and looked at it. *If the Defense Intelligence Agency would not help her, this will be an option,* Wynne thought. She tucked the card into her purse.

## *Chapter Twelve*

*March, 1986*

DURING THE FLIGHT to Washington, Wynne continued to glance through a copy of the *Atlanta Constitution*, which she had picked up during her layover in Atlanta.  It was hard to concentrate on anything, but an article with the dateline Bangkok, Thailand caught her eye.  A news release from the State Department advised that United States, Vietnamese and Cambodian officials were to meet on the coming Friday and Saturday in Phnom Penh, the capital of Cambodia, to discuss joint procedures for resolving cases of Americans missing along the Cambodia-Vietnam border. *Why not those lost along the North Vietnam border, too*? She tore the item from the newspaper, and put it in her purse to discuss with Colonel Hale. Jason had taught her to question people in authority.

As the plane circled over the Washington area to land at Dulles airport, the scene below brought back many memories. Wynne thought back to the trip so many years ago when she flew to Washington for the Congressional Medal of Honor ceremony. The Washington Monument and Lincoln Memorial stood out like white beacons below as she had remembered them from her earlier trip. The dome of the Capitol still glistened in the sunlight.

She looked for the Vietnam Veterans Memorial, which she had visited on numerous occasions since it was dedicated in 1982. She could see its thin black silhouette nestled between the Washington Monument and the Lincoln Memorial. How many times had she stood at that wall and traced her fingers over the name *Michael J Reardon*? She could feel his presence as her fingers moved over the cold, black granite. *How she had longed for that presence!* The Memorial had been described by the media as an artistic abstraction. *Michael's name on the wall was no abstraction...it was a reality she found hard to accept.*

As the plane circled to land, Wynne saw the unique structure of the Dulles Airport Terminal building. After the plane landed, she gathered her belongings, and made her way to the waiting room to meet Stephen.

"Over here, Mother!" Stephen called. She then saw him standing by the boarding counter. Her heart quickened when she saw his smile. It was so much like his father's.

He embraced her warmly and said, "It's so good to see you."

"You, too," she said as she kissed him on the cheek.

"How's Jason?" he asked. "Is his pottery studio in Pensacola doing well, and still keeping the Gallery in the black?"

Wynne smiled and said, "Yes he is doing fine. He sends his best."

As they claimed her luggage, Stephen tentatively broached the reason for her Washington visit.

"Mother, I hope your conversation with Colonel Hale will finally put this to rest for you."

As he spoke he grabbed her suitcase from the luggage carousel.

A look of determination flashed in Wynne's eyes. "I hope it will do more than put it to rest, Stephen. I hope this will give us some real leads we can follow."

Stephen just shook his head, and accompanied his mother to the parking garage.

As they exited the Dulles terminal area on to the Dulles Access Highway, Wynne asked, "Could we please stop by the Memorial?"

"Of course," Stephen said with a smile. It was expected that anytime his mother was in the Washington area the Vietnam Veterans Memorial would be her first stop.

As they drove toward the Memorial, Stephen asked, "What do you expect to learn from Colonel Hale?"

"I want his assurance that they are following all of the leads that would explain that photograph," his mother replied.

"Mom, you're getting your hopes up needlessly," Stephen said, reaching for her hand. "This has all been covered before. Please accept the truth...Dad is dead."

"But the photograph...the records in Moscow. There surely has to be an explanation ..." she replied.

"Mom, it's been 14 years." Stephen's voice softened. "You have to let it go."

Wynne looked out of the window as they drove by the Lincoln Memorial. "Let's reserve judgment until we talk with Colonel Hale," she said.

Stephen parked in a lot near the Vietnam Veterans Memorial. They joined others who were in silent meditation at the Memorial. The polished black wall always took her breath away with the almost 58,000 names engraved on it. The flowers and other memorabilia laid lovingly against the wall were poignant reminders of the enormity of the losses of American lives Vietnam had caused, and of the overwhelming grief individual families still had to bear.

They paused at the flag pole on the path to the Memorial, and read the inscription at its base: *This flag represents the service rendered to our country by the veterans of the Vietnam War. The flag affirms the principles of freedom for which they fought and their pride in having served under difficult circumstances.* Seals of all of the Armed Services encircled the inscription, and the American flag fluttered above in the cold winter wind.

Wynne remembered the somber occasion of the groundbreaking of the Memorial in 1982.

Congressmen, senators, family members, and friends had stood under umbrellas on a rainy day, and paid tribute to the proposed Memorial designed by an American architect, Maya Lin. The names of 58,000 American servicemen, who died in Southeast Asia, would be inscribed on the black granite wall. She cringed as she remembered the anti-war statement at the time that cited the wall as a "black wall of shame". She had stood with the others and listened as Secretary of Defense Richard Cheney praised the brave men and women who gave their lives for their country.

Stephen gently tugged at her sleeve, and returned her thoughts to the present. "Mom," he said gently. "Let's go to the Wall."

Wynne and Stephen then stopped in front of the panel with Michael's name. She traced her fingers over the letters of *Michael J. Reardon*. *If only this were not true*, she thought in anguish. She could imagine the reflection of Michael's blue eyes looking at her from the wall - those same intense blue eyes that she saw in the recent photograph. *How could it not be him?*

Janet Morgan had been quite convincing, but surely the Defense Intelligence Agency could track down other leads now that there was confirmation, even if they did feel that the photograph was fraudulent. And Boris Yeltsin's admission certainly gave extra credence to the possibility that Michael could still be alive. *The business card in her purse for the Operation Recovery Agency also held some hope for a search.*

"I guess we'd better go to the Pentagon," she said, looking back at the wall with a feeling of enormous loss in her heart.

Stephen's eyes clouded with tears as he took her by the arm, and they left the Memorial.

***

WYNNE AND STEPHEN were met in the lobby of the Pentagon by Colonel Hale's aide. The sight of a blue Air Force uniform, which had given her such an overwhelming feeling of sadness after Michael's death, now gave only delightful memories as she recalled how handsome he looked in his uniform.

"This way please," the young man said in a clipped voice. He accompanied them to the Defense Intelligence Agency's office located on the third floor.

A security guard saluted smartly as they entered the office where they were met by the

Colonel. The rather young looking officer stood ramrod straight as he greeted them and then ushered them into his office. His intense blue eyes and military bearing reminded her of Michael.

"Mrs. Reardon...I'm Colonel Hale."

"This is my son Stephen. He has some questions, too."

"Of course. Please have a seat...both of you." He motioned to the straight back chairs positioned in front of his desk.

Wynne and Stephen sat across the desk from the officer. A sense of anticipation overcame her, but it was tempered by a feeling of dread. *She just couldn't lose Michael a second time.* Stephen, sensing his mother's anguish, reached over and patted her gently on the arm.

"I'm pleased to see that President Bush has sent a representative to Moscow to investigate the assertions by President Yeltsin," she said.

"Mrs. Reardon, we have been investigating all of these leads regarding Vietnam MIAs and POWs that are coming from the Russians. The chairman of the Russian parliamentary commission that oversees the archives of the KGB has promised his complete support. He has invited American historians to search their documents that could reveal the fate of Americans taken prisoner during the Vietnam War. We are appointing a committee to go to Moscow to do this next month." He paused and added, somewhat reluctantly, "But some of the Soviet records are up to 50 years old, and have probably been altered through the years by those who do not want to leave a trail of their actions. So these files may be suspect."

"What about the recent news report that some American POWs were taken to Russia?" Wynne asked.

"Yes, Mrs. Reardon...our intelligence files do show that U.S. airmen who were shot down over Korea during the Korean War were incarcerated in labor camps or mental hospitals in Russia ... but Vietnam pilots? No. There is no information to support such a theory...I'm sorry."

Unshed tears burned Wynne's eyes as the Colonel continued.

The Colonel sighed. "I wish it were that simple in Major Reardon's case, but it's my sad duty to inform you that your husband's death in 1972 was confirmed by indigenous sources. Many of these stories we're hearing now of MIAs and POWs still alive in Southeast Asia have no basis in fact." Colonel Hale continued to speak in a detached manner.

"But the photograph...the newspaper is dated two years ago," Wynne insisted.

"The photograph has been altered as I explained to Chaplain Turner...perhaps altered and superimposed with a newspaper of a more recent date. We suspect you will be asked for money to fund a search for Major Reardon. Please notify us if you are."

Wynne reached in her purse and took out the business card of the Operation Recovery Agency. *How could they prey on desperate families? Such actions would be unconscionable.* She started to hand the card to Colonel Hale, and then placed it back it her purse. *It was now her only hope of finding Michael.*

"But why is our government not meeting with officials from North Vietnam like the conference with officials from Cambodia?" Wynne asked, her mind numb with what the Colonel insisted was true.

"The Russian government has sent representatives to North Vietnam to seek release of information on American servicemen. And when we get the KGB files and those of the Russian Defense Ministry we have been promised, perhaps there will be an explanation for some of the other cases. Some deserters from Vietnam did go to Russia. There will be hearings on this in the fall in

Moscow. That may explain the fate of some MIAs and POWs, but Major Reardon did not go to Russia, nor was he interrogated recently." His voice softened. "Mrs. Reardon, Major Reardon has not been a MIA or a POW. He died on that Vietnamese hillside in 1972. I'm very sorry."

"Why haven't we been better informed about the matter?" Stephen asked.

The Colonel stood and paused beside his desk. "Much of the MIA/POW information is classified. We are not at liberty to discuss it."

"Even with families?" Wynne asked.

"Especially with families, Mrs. Reardon. I'm very sorry that I cannot tell you anything more."

With those words, Wynne and Stephen stood to leave. Wynne perfunctorily thanked the Colonel for his time. As she left the Pentagon, she knew her next step would be to contact the Operation Recovery Agency. They would be her last hope to find Michael. *The $10,000 would be the best investment she ever made.*

Wynne and Stephen stopped at the Georgian Manor in Georgetown for dinner. It had been a Washington landmark, and was one of Michael's favorite restaurants. The waiter seated them in a quiet corner, and handed them menus and a wine list.

When Wynne looked over the menu selections, she smiled. She could hear Michael's order, "*Salmon en brioche.*" The gourmet dish was still on the menu after all of these years.

"What will you have tonight, Mother?" Stephen asked, his blue eyes sparkling in the candlelight.

"Your father's favorite, of course...*Salmon en brioche.*"

"Is it really that good?" he asked.

"Yes it is. The crust is so flaky it melts in your mouth..." Her voice trailed off as memories of earlier dinners there with Michael engulfed her.

After the waiter took their order and brought two glasses of iced tea, Stephen looked at his mother intently.

"Mother, can't you just let this go? The information on Dad's death is pretty conclusive. Please stop this continuing pain, and get on with your life. You have Jason now...he loves you...he wants to marry you,...and he is alive." Stephen then added softly, "And, Mom, Jason has always been there for all of us." He reached across the table and clasped her hand. She squeezed his tightly.

"Stephen, you'll just never understand. I can't let go until they either find your father alive, or identify his remains. Closing the door completely on this without that proof can never be an option. I hope that you and Lauren can understand that some day."

They ate their meal in virtual silence. Stephen commented on how delicious the *Salmon en Brioche* was, and Wynne merely nodded in agreement.

After dinner they drove to Stephen's Georgetown apartment.

"When will Lauren receive her Master's Degree?" Stephen asked as they sat in his living room, and he poured his mother a cup of coffee.

"She's planning on graduating June 6th," Wynne replied. She's working on her thesis prospectus on the roots of the Vietnam conflict. She just completed a course in Human Conflict: Theory and Resolution. She decided to pursue that area in regard to Vietnam, and explore what could have been done differently for a peaceful resolution of that conflict."

"Sounds like quite a thesis project," Stephen said. "But knowing my little sister, she'll handle it well."

"Yes, she will," Wynne agreed. "She's been quite a student of the Vietnam conflict ever since she started her Master's Degree program in International Relations."

"I know that she has some definite opinions about the South Vietnam government. She said that all of her studies showed that the government was unstable and corrupt. I share her concern on how we could have supported them as an ally."

"Your father would have disagreed with Lauren. He felt their independence should have been supported, and said that we were trying to keep them independent from Ho Chi Minh's government."

"I know he would have, Mom. Lauren's Master's in International Relations should certainly open some career doors for her. I would imagine the State Department would welcome someone with her knowledge to analyze strategies and techniques for the peaceful resolution of conflict."

"I certainly hope so," Wynne said. "But she indicated an interest in working for an international organization, or perhaps living abroad. She has quite an adventuresome spirit, you know."

"Yes I know," Stephen said, thinking about the unbridled enthusiasm Lauren always expressed about life.

They finished their coffee without any further reference to Wynne's visit to see Colonel Hale.

"I guess I'd better call it a day," Wynne said, as she put her cup and saucer on the counter.

"Goodnight, Mother, I'll see you in the morning," Stephen replied, as he kissed her on the cheek.

Wynne went into her room and called Jason. His vibrant voice on the other end of the line always lifted her spirits.

"Colonel Hale is convinced that Michael died on that Vietnamese hillside," Wynne said simply.

"Colonel Hale should know," Jason said. He paused and the added, "Wynne, please listen to him..."

*You sound like Stephen*, Wynne thought before she said simply, "I'll see you tomorrow."

\*\*\*

THE NEXT DAY after a warm good-bye embrace from Stephen, Wynne boarded the plane for the flight home. Her seat mate gave her a copy of the *Washington Star*. "Pilots on Wall alive" the newspaper headline proclaimed. She quickly read the article. Two names on the Vietnam Veterans Memorial wall had been found to be in error. Both pilots were still alive. Somehow their military records had been misfiled and they were declared K.I.A. *If their names were put on the wall in error, why not Michael's, too?* She looked out of the window at the bright sunlight striking the wing of the plane.

*I'll send this article to Colonel Hale,* she thought as she tore it from the newspaper. The trip home then seemed much faster than the flight to Washington. Wynne knew that as soon as she contacted the Agency, a search would be on for Michael. *A blonde, blue-eyed American living in Vietnam surely would not be too hard to find.*

***

JASON MET WYNNE'S plane at the Pensacola airport. He was a sympathetic listener as she told him of the Air Force's continued insistence that Michael was dead.

"Wynne, perhaps you should listen to them," he said as they drove over the Bay Bridge. "They did have in-country sources to confirm losses...I think you're in for a terrible let down."

Wynne's entire body tensed. "As long as there is no body...proof that Michael is dead...there is still hope," she said tersely.

"All right, Wynne. As I promised you earlier...we'll see this through together," Jason assured, but with an air of resignation.

\*\*\*

LAUREN CAME HOME for the weekend, and found the clipping on the breakfast table the next morning. She shook her head as she read it. "Oh, Mom," she murmured. She dialed Stephen's office number in Washington.

He answered quickly. "Hi, it's me," Lauren said. "How are you?"

"Hello, Lauren. I'm fine. How's Mom?"

"That's why I'm calling. Did you read about the Vietnam War veterans who are very much alive even though their names are on the Memorial wall?"

"No, I didn't. I guess that has Mom full of more hope."

"Yes, I'm afraid so. Could you talk to Colonel Hale about it? Mom is sending him the clipping, although I'm sure it's general knowledge there."

Stephen sighed. "Sure, Lauren, but I already know what he'll say."

"I know," Lauren said softly. "Thank you...talk to you later."

Stephen dialed Colonel Hale's number at the Pentagon. The crisp voice answered, "Colonel Hale's office."

"Stephen Reardon calling for Colonel Hale, please."

"Yes, Sir. One moment please."

The Colonel was immediately on the line.

"Sir, this is Stephen Reardon. I'm calling regarding the news that two Vietnam veterans whose names are on the wall are alive. How do you explain that?"

There was momentary silence on the other end of the line. "Well, Mr. Reardon, the State Department is making a statement about that soon. I'm afraid I cannot comment."

"You realize this gives my mother further confirmation that Dad may be alive."

Colonel Hale's voice softened as he said, "Son, she really shouldn't use that incident to keep her hopes alive. There's no comparison to the situations."

Stephen paused and said, "I'm very sorry to hear that."

"I am, too," Colonel Hale replied.

Stephen put the receiver down with an air or resignation. *Would it never end?* His thoughts were interrupted by the ringing of the telephone. He answered crisply, "Delcom, Stephen Reardon."

***

STEPHEN AND LAUREN were both home to visit with their mother the next weekend. Lauren invited Jason to join them for dinner in the hopes he could help them convince their mother to give up her quest to find their father, who the military still insisted was dead.

Lauren finished setting the dinner table with the earthenware from the Gallery that had been made by the previous potter. The pieces were of museum quality.

"Not too bad," Jason said as he balanced a bronzed colored dinner plate on his palm.

'You're just jealous of Anna's ability as a potter," Lauren teased with a laugh. She retrieved the plate from Jason's hand, and put it back on the table.

Jason's brown eyes flashed a defiant look. "I will give her credit for making passable pottery," he said with a wink.

"I guess her wall of Blue Ribbons has already done that," Wynne said as she placed a steaming casserole in the center of the table.

"You called?" Stephen asked, sticking his head into the dining room.

"No, but you're just in time," his mother said.

"What's happening at school?" Jason asked as he passed the seafood casserole dish to Lauren.

'We're learning why the Vietnam War was a source of conflict rather than consensus for Americans," she responded.

Jason had a bemused expression on his face. "You don't need a graduate course in International Relations to answer that question. Just ask any Vietnam vet."

"OK...so why was it a source of conflict here at home?" Stephen asked as he scooped some salad into his salad bowl.

"Well the first thing is that the war was never declared, and our military objectives were never clear," Jason responded.

"Wasn't the daily TV coverage a problem, too?" Wynne asked as she poured glasses of iced tea. "It was certainly a problem for me."

"Of course," he replied. "It was a daily reminder of what was going on...especially of our losses. Remember...the United States had no clear victories at any time during the war, according to the television coverage."

"I think the South Vietnam government was a big problem, too," Lauren said. "Everything I've studied about them shows that it was unstable and corrupt. How could we have supported them as an ally?"

"We were trying to keep them independent from Ho Chi Minh's government," Stephen said. "Hey, this is a great seafood casserole, Mom. I don't get this good seafood in D.C."

"Thanks, Stephen...Lauren, I think your father would have disagreed with you about the South Vietnamese government."

'I know, Mom," Lauren said, reaching across the table, and patting her mother's hand.

Wynne resisted all attempts to get her to end the search for Michael as they discussed it while dinner progressed.

"Can't we just enjoy the fact that both of you are home for the weekend and enjoy dinner?" she pleaded.

Stephen, Lauren, and Jason all hid their disappointment at their failure to get Wynne to face the truth.

## *Chapter Thirteen*

*March, 1986*

WYNNE CALLED THE number on the Operation Recovery Agency's business card from her office at the Gallery the next morning. A quick response on the other end made her hopes soar.

"This is Wynne Reardon," she said. "I'd like to begin a search for my husband in Vietnam."

A friendly voice on the other end of the line responded. "Certainly, Mrs. Reardon...that is our mission. Was your husband declared missing or taken prisoner?"

She hesitated momentarily. "No, he was presumed to be killed in action on the North Vietnam border in December 1972, but I have acquired a recent photograph of him taken in December of last year. I believe he's still alive."

"Well, we will do everything possible to verify that," the voice said. "My name is Gordon Wells. I was an officer in Vietnam, and am coordinating this effort. You do understand that there is a fee of $10,000 to cover search expenses. And with the recent information coming out of Russia, our inquiries will also take us into Moscow to review those KGB documents."

"I'll send a copy of the photograph, and a Cashier's check tomorrow," Wynne said with her heart pounding.

"That will be fine. We'll start our search immediately. Just let me get a few details about your husband. His full name, rank at the time he was in Vietnam, and the circumstances of the December 1972 event."

Wynne was encouraged that he used the term, event, not your husband's reported death. "It's Major Michael James Reardon. His plane went down on the North Vietnam border while he was protecting a fellow crew member's plane. His body was never recovered, but the Air Force is insisting that he is dead. He was awarded the Congressional Medal of Honor posthumously..." Her voice trailed off as she stifled a sob.

Gordon Wells' voice seemed to soften. "I understand, Mrs. Reardon. We'll be in touch as

271

soon as there is any news. We'll try to keep you apprised on a weekly basis, unless there is some breaking news earlier than that."

"That will be fine," Wynne said. "I'll look forward to hearing from you."

She looked at her calendar, and noted that it was March 6th. *How long would it be before she heard from this Agency?*

*** 

AS WYNNE AWAITED word from the Agency, the memories she had tried to put aside of America's involvement in Vietnam all came back. Michael's patriotism had never wavered, but Jason had explained to her how the noble purpose of the Vietnam War -- to keep the people of South Vietnam out of the Communist sphere -- had been lost in the politics that had replaced military strategy. "America's policy of gradualism," he had said bitterly, "cost us 58,000 lives."

*If Michael were dead, had he died because of senseless political restrictions?* She could not let herself accept that. She clung to the belief that he had helped make the world a better place to live.

\*\*\*

**A WEEK AFTER** her first contact with the Operation Recovery Agency, she received a letter from them.

> *Dear Mrs. Reardon:*
>
> *We have received the photograph and check. We have just learned that Soviet Intelligence interviewed Americans in Vietnam as recently as last year. We feel that access to their records will be quite valuable. We look forward to helping you find your loved one.*
>
> *Sincerely,*
>
> *Gordon Wells, Coordinator*
> *Operation Recovery Agency*

Later in the day she also received a telephone call from Gordon Wells.

"Mrs. Reardon."

"Yes ..." Wynne said, as her heart raced.

"We have confirmed Major Reardon's body was never found, so that gives us some hope. We have a team of historians in Moscow now going through the KGB files. If there are any leads, they will find them. We'll let you know."

"Thank you," Wynne said, encouraged by the news. "And the photograph?"

"We're working on that. We have a photography lab examining it at this very moment. We'll keep you informed."

After she hung up the telephone, she hurried to the pottery area where Jason was glazing some pieces he had brought from his studio.

"It's great to see you looking so happy," he said. "To what do we owe that smile?"

She explained her contact with the Operation Recovery Agency and Gordon Wells' findings.

"Who is Gordon Wells?" asked Jason.

"He was an officer who served in Vietnam."

"How old is this Operation Recovery Agency?" Jason asked.

"I don't know, but he appears to have all the necessary international connections." Wynne heard her exaggeration of the facts, and felt ashamed. *She didn't need to justify her contact with Gordon Wells. She had no choice but to seek their professional help.*

"That certainly adds credibility to his operation," Jason said quietly.

*Did he sound sarcastic?*

"It does what?" Wynne asked.

He did not answer and walked away with a reflective look on his face.

***

WYNNE TRIED TO resume a normal schedule at the Gallery, but it was hard for her to concentrate. She found herself frequently looking at the telephone, willing it to ring. When it finally did ring, she was so startled she spilled the contents of her out basket.

The Gallery's secretary, Connie Evans, came on the intercom.

"Wynne, it's Gordon Wells for you," Connie said.

Wynne took a deep breath as she reached for the receiver.

"Mr. Wells..."

"Mrs. Reardon, we do have some news that I thought you should know about as soon as possible...It's not definitive, but encouraging."

Wynne's pulse quickened. "Yes...?"

"It has just come to our attention that some construction engineers from Yugoslavia were working on a project in North Vietnam last year when they were taken on a bus ride into the country. The bus became lost on a winding road. As the driver stopped for information, they saw some Caucasians working in a field...A bus passenger counted about twelve. One of the field workers, who appeared to be an American in his mid-fifties, approached the bus."

"Were they able to get his name?" Wynne asked.

"No...the bus driver drove away before the engineers had a chance to talk with the man. But the mere fact that there are Caucasians in North Vietnam working in the fields is encouraging. It means that we if we contact one of them, we may be able to trace Major Reardon's whereabouts," Wells said.

Wynne was elated by the excitement in Gordon Wells' voice. The story matched the incident Lauren's professor had told her about Caucasian prisoners being seen in North Vietnam!

"How soon can you contact them?" Wynne asked.

"The engineers can provide us an approximate route of their bus trip. We have people in-country who can take it from there. I'll be in touch as soon as we have some more information. I must tell you, Mrs. Reardon, you have come on board with our Agency at a very exciting time."

"Thank you," Wynne said, almost breathless. The agony of waiting for word on Michael now was as hard as it had been when he was shot down in December 1972. She had held out hope then beyond the time the Air Force said that she should. But her optimism that he might still be alive was sustained by the fervent belief that he could have survived almost anything if put to the test. He had promised to return safely. *She still believed he would.*

Jason came into the office to give her an invoice for his pottery just as she hung up the telephone. She explained the circumstances of the Caucasians reportedly seen in North Vietnam.

"That sounds a bit far-fetched, Wynne," he said, his dark brows etched with concern. "I can't imagine that the 2300 Americans, who are still listed as missing in action in Vietnam, are working in the fields in North Vietnam."

"He didn't say there were thousands," Wynne snapped, her eyes flashing in anger. "The engineers estimated that there were about a dozen. Michael could be one of them."

Jason paused and said, "I know how much you want them to find Michael," he said. "But you have to accept the reality of the situation."

"You sound just like Colonel Hale," she accused. "You have your own reality."

"We must consider both sides," Jason said.

***

TWO WEEKS LATER Wynne received a letter from the Agency.

*Dear Mrs. Reardon:*

*Our research to date on the possible location of your husband, Major Michael Reardon, is quite promising. We have uncovered records in the Soviet Files that* *lead us to believe that he indeed was taken to Russia in the mid-seventies. We have other leads that we need to pursue, but this quest will require additional funding. I'm sure that you understand that international travel is quite expensive, and information of this nature has a premium price, but we don't want to give up now when we feel that we're so close. We ask that you send an additional $6,000 as soon as possible. We will continue our search with great diligence.*

*Sincerely,*
*Gordon Wells, Coordinator*
*Operation Recovery Agency*

*How could she get Jason to sign for a second mortgage on the Gallery for the money?* Then Wynne remembered he usually signed all of the requests for supplies with barely a glance.

Later that day she obtained a form from the bank to request a second mortgage of $6,000 on the Gallery. She filled out the information, placed the form in a stack of requisitions for Jason's signature, and left them in his mail box.

Wynne was writing a letter to a purchaser of a commissioned fiber piece when Jason stuck his head in the door and handed her the stack of requisitions.

"I'm sure you're looking for these," he said with a smile.

"Yes, I am." She took them from him without further comment.

*** 

WYNNE FINGERED THE handle of her purse as the bank's loan officer, Bob Lawrence, looked over the Gallery's financial records.

"This Gallery has become a very successful operation," Mr. Lawrence said with a smile.

"Yes, it has," Wynne replied. "Our excellent potter made the difference."

"And you want a second mortgage of $6,000? Is that correct?" he asked.

"Yes," Wynne replied.

"I see that that the Gallery is a partnership, and that Mr. Garrison agrees with the second mortgage."

Wynne visibly flinched. She remembered when she and Jason had set up the partnership for the Gallery, and he had questioned if they shouldn't incorporate instead. Wynne had replied at the time that she trusted him to take care of the children's interests, and incorporation wasn't necessary.

"Yes...he agrees," Wynne said now more curtly than she had intended.

"May I ask how you plan to use the money?"

"I assure you that it is a critical expenditure."

"Well," Mr. Lawrence, said as he signed the loan papers. "I won't question your judgment. But remember you have put your Gallery at risk with a second mortgage."

Wynne nodded. She understood the risk, but felt she had no other choice. *Michael's life -- or death -- may be the real risk here. If it meant that she would find Michael, then nothing else mattered.*

"It will take just a moment to cut the check," the bank officer said. "I'll be right back."

Wynne's mouth felt dry when she said, "Thank you." She tried to imagine what it would be like to find Michael at last, to catch up on those lost years. *Nothing else would ever matter again.*

\*\*\*

WYNNE RECEIVED ANOTHER telephone call from Gordon Wells on Saturday.

"Mrs. Reardon, our historians have found Major Reardon's name in the KGB documents in Moscow. He apparently was interrogated in the mid-seventies."

The news was like electricity surging through her body. Wynne felt euphoric. *Colonel Hale and the Defense Intelligence Agency were wrong! Michael was possibly still in Vietnam, or perhaps even in Russia.*

"How soon can you verify the documents?" she asked when she had caught her breath.

"We'll send this information to our people in Saigon," Gordon Wells said. "They should be able to visit the location of the interrogations, and find where the Americans were sent from there. We're getting closer, Mrs. Reardon."

"Thank you...such exciting news! I'll look forward to hearing from you." Wynne laid the receiver in its cradle as though it might break, and leaned back in her chair. She felt lifted on the wings of a million butterflies.

She sensed a twinge of guilt that she hadn't shared the payment of an additional $6,000 with Stephen, Lauren, and Jason, but she couldn't stand their skepticism and disapproval. They could never understand why she was willing to put the Gallery at risk with a second mortgage.

Stephen called early on Monday morning. "Mother, how are you? I assume there are no new developments from the Agency that's looking for Dad, since you haven't called."

"Well, not exactly," Wynne said with some hesitation.

"What do you mean 'not exactly'?" Stephen asked.

"They do have some leads, Stephen. They needed some more money to continue the search. I sent them an additional $6,000 last week."

"Mother!" Stephen's voice exploded in her ear. "I can't believe you've done that. What did you use? All of Dad's life insurance...and Jason let you do this?"

"No...he doesn't know that I took out a second mortgage on the Gallery. It will be all right. They will find your father."

"You lied to Jason?" Stephen's voice then softened. "Mom, they will never find Dad. Please let it go."

"I can't," Wynne said softly as she hung up the telephone. *Why did everyone have to be so doubtful that Michael could be found? Didn't they have evidence the Russians did take POWs to Moscow? Michael could well be one of them. She just had to believe that.*

\*\*\*

JASON CIRCLED THE date in an article that he was reading in the *Vietnam Veterans Against the War Journal.* The article was titled "Caucasians on Collective Farm in North Vietnam." Yet the date that they were reported seen was 1980, a full five years before Gordon Wells of the Operation Recovery Agency had said it had happened.

*That's where the good coordinator got this piece of fiction that he told Wynne,* Jason thought. *I'll just have to see what other fabrication he'll try to come up with for her.*

Jason decided to call one of the veterans who had served with him in Vietnam to inquire about the Operation Recovery Agency.

"Josh, it's Jason Garrison...Yes, it has been a long time."

"Where are you, Buddy?" Josh asked. "I kinda lost track after we left 'Nam."

"I'm working at a gallery in Northwest Florida now. I've called to see if you know anything about the Operation Recovery Agency...They reportedly search for MIAs and POWs in Vietnam."

"Yeah, reportedly is the operative word there. Their big search is for the big bucks," Josh said.

"You're saying that they aren't a legitimate operation?"

"That's what I'm saying. And you aren't the first person to ask me about them either. Ron Chandler's wife paid them $10,000 when she received a photograph that looked similar to Ron, even though he was reported killed on the Cambodian border in February of 1972. His Phantom was hit by enemy ground fire, and the plane exploded in mid-air. There was no way they could find him alive...nobody could have survived. Excavations in the eighties turned up his remains and aircraft wreckage, and proved those Agency folks who sent that picture were crooks."

"Thank you, Josh. I'm going to see what I can do to stop this kind of emotional and financial exploitation."

"It's about time that somebody stopped them...let me know if I can help."

Jason then called the Defense Intelligence Agency's office and asked for Colonel Hale. The officer quickly came on the line.

"Colonel Hale, this is Jason Garrison. I'm calling on behalf of Wynne Reardon to see if you have been able to obtain any information on the KGB files."

"Yes, Mr. Garrison. I was planning to call Mrs. Reardon later today, pending receipt of written verification. Our team going over the KGB files has failed to find any record of Major Reardon. I'm sure that Mrs. Reardon will receive a request for money from one of the fraudulent search groups." He paused. "I'm sorry our information isn't more positive."

"Thank you," Jason said, as he hung up the telephone angrier than he had been since he had protested government duplicity as a leader of Vietnam Veterans Against the War. These impostors had given Wynne false hope, and undermined her security. *When should he tell her? Perhaps he should wait until she heard from Colonel Hale.*

***

IN LESS THAN a week, Wynne had another call from Gordon Wells.

"Mrs. Reardon, we've located a photograph of the wreckage of your husband's plane. We have confirmed in-country reports that the pilot of this particular plane did survive the crash and was taken prisoner. We have natives who were eyewitnesses. They will reveal even more information for money. This is, of course, unfortunate, but the way we must work in Vietnam these days."

"What type of plane is it?" Wynne asked.

"It's a F-105 fighter," Gordon Wells answered.

"F-105?" Wynne said. "I told you he was flying a F-4 Phantom." Her chest tightened. *How could this Agency make such a mistake?*

"Oh, of course," Gordon Wells said quickly. "I'm sorry. It was thinking about another incident. Please forgive me. It is a photograph of a F-4 Phantom. I'll send a copy to you in the next mail."

"Yes, please do," Wynne said quietly, catching her lower lip between her teeth to stop its trembling. *Maybe the misidentification of the plane was an innocent error, after all.*

\*\*\*

GORDON WELLS SAT transfixed as overheads of POW sites in Vietnam came into view. "Too bad they moved everyone to Hanoi after the botched POW rescue at Son Tay," Wells said.

"Yeah, there were some disappointed Special Forces when they found an empty prison compound. We can use these old identified sites in our correspondence and telephone conversations with families though," his aide, Kirk Logan, said. "These will add credibility because the locations have a paper trail in our government archives."

"The Agency needs more than a paper trail for credibility," Wells said with a frown.

"But we have people in-country," his aide assured. "They will back up any story about MIAs and POWs we want to promote."

"I certainly hope so. We're paying those beggars in North Vietnam an exorbitant amount of money. It's this Moscow Bound stuff we've really got to substantiate. Now that Russia has opened their archives, we can really promote this theory of American servicemen taken to Russia."

"Yes, but that was primarily POWs during the Korean War," Logan explained.

"But the families of Vietnam servicemen don't know that," Wells said with a smile. "They'll shell out $10,000 without hesitation thinking their husbands or sons might be in Moscow. This news is a godsend for our company. Just imagine how much mileage we can get out of this current press!" Gordon Wells laughed and stubbed out a cigar in his ashtray.

***

LATER THAT EVENING Gordon Wells met several of his Vietnam buddies at the Asian Restaurant in Arlington. As Wells regaled his buddies with war stories, he laughed and said, "Widow Reardon is going to be a gold mine! I think she's good for another $6,000."

"Beats selling through the black market in Saigon, don't it?" an aide Gerald Marshall said.

Wells eyes narrowed and he pounded on the table with his fist. "Don't you ever mention that again!"

Marshall looked startled. "Hey, Buddy. Take it easy. No harm intended." He looked warily at his colleague.

Wells simply glowered at him and didn't respond.

***

"WYNNE, I NEED to talk with you," Jason said, sitting down on the sofa in her office.

She tensed. *Had Jason discovered the second mortgage?*

"Certainly, Jason...some problem with the Gallery?"

"No, Wynne, it's about the Operation Recovery Agency."

"Oh, they should contact me again soon," she said, beaming with excitement. "They have a photograph of Michael's downed plane, and some eyewitnesses who may lead them to the interrogation site in Vietnam. They think they can follow the paper trail to find Michael."

Jason took her hands in his. "Wynne, there is no paper trail for Michael."

Wynne jerked her hands away. "What do you mean? The historians in Moscow found Michael's name in the documents there. He was interrogated in the mid-seventies. They will be able to find him. And the engineers saw those Caucasians in the fields in North Vietnam last year. Michael could be one of them."

"Wynne, those Caucasians were seen in the fields in North Vietnam in 1980, not in 1985. A recent article in my *VVAW Journal* confirms that. And about the Agency itself... A friend of mine said that the agency took $10,000 from a widow to find her husband when the body had been positively identified years ago. There's a cottage industry of prisoner-hunters out there now. There's no one more vulnerable to this scam than a grieving family, who will clutch at any straws to find a loved one they believe to be alive..."

"But if there's even a thread of hope that Michael is alive, I have to try." Wynne's eyes flashed a look of determination, even a look of warning. "Don't do this, Jason..."

"I have to," he said gently, "There's more..."

"And the KGB documents?" she asked, choking back tears.

"Michael's name is not in the KGB documents according to Colonel Hale. Wynne...accept the facts. Michael is dead... I'll call the FBI for you."

Wynne nodded and tears flowed down her cheeks as Jason went to the telephone and dialed information. "The FBI office," he said.

"Hello, Federal Bureau of Investigation," a crisp voice answered on the first ring.

"This is Jason Garrison. I need to report a fraudulent Agency who is taking advantage of a Vietnam widow."

***

THE FOLLOWING SATURDAY Wynne and Jason had an appointment at the Gallery from FBI agent, Douglas Warren. As she ushered him into her office, he said, "We've learned Gordon Wells received a General Discharge for trafficking in the black market while he was a Lieutenant in Vietnam. He should have been court-martialed and put in prison, but getting him out of the service was the best the military could do. He'll serve time now though for this fraud. You're not the only widow he's taken money from. We've got him this time -- Wells and his associate."

"How could he..." Wynne asked indignantly, fists clinched at her side.

"Those crooks have no shame, Mrs. Reardon. And prison is too good for them."

"I wanted their promises to be true, don't you..." Wynne explained, looking at Agent Warren.

"It would have been a miracle if their claims were true," he said softly. "We'll need all of your correspondence from the Operation Recovery Agency and your canceled checks. And you will have to testify in Federal Court."

"I have everything here in this envelope," Wynne assured.

"At last these people are finally going to have some accountability," Jason said, clenching his fists. "I just talked to the Inspector General's office. They wanted a deposition from me, too. If it were up to me, I'd line the whole bunch up against the wall and shoot them -- and I thought I had become a pacifist after the war."

"They'll get substantial time in a Federal Prison," Agent Warren assured.

"Yes, but that won't return the money to the families they swindled or help with the pain that Agency put them through," Jason said, his eyes showing anger.

"Knowing Gordon Wells can never do this to anyone else gives me some peace," Wynne said, as she handed the records to the agent.

Jason nodded and flashed a quick smile to her. "I'm glad," his lips said soundlessly.

Douglas Warren stood to leave. "I'm sorry we didn't catch them before they found you, Mrs. Reardon. I appreciate your help in stopping their heartless scam. I hope we can get some of your money back."

As the door closed behind the agent, Wynne said, "It's like giving Michael up all over again," as she continued to weep.

"We'll get through this together," Jason assured, taking her into his arms.

***

THE NEXT WEEK Wynne received a call from the State Attorney General. "Mrs. Reardon, it's Nathan Randolph. I'm a Vietnam veteran and quite interested in this recovery agency you dealt with to search for your husband."

"All of that will come out in the Federal trial," Wynne said. "I don't know what more I can add."

"Well, if you could just give me the date you first contacted them that would be a great help."

"It was March 6th," Wynne said.

"Thank you," Nathan Randolph said. "I'll be in touch again later."

*What is that all about?* Wynne hung up the phone rather puzzled about the call.

\*\*\*

THE COURTROOM IN the Federal Court House in Pensacola was hushed as Wynne testified against the Operation Recovery Agency. The federal prosecutor gently led her through the questions about her husband's status as KIA, body not recovered. Colonel Hale testified that there was never any doubt that Major Michael Reardon was killed in action on a Vietnamese hillside on December 23, 1972. It was readily apparent the Agency's attempts to find him alive were fraudulent.

The jury's verdict was swift and decisive. The verdict, "Guilty, Your Honor," for both Wells and Logan echoed through the courtroom. They were each sentenced to 10 years in Federal prison. As Jason and Wynne left the Court House, a barrage of reporters and photographers stopped them.

"Do you feel justice was served, Mrs. Reardon?" one reporter asked.

As he spoke, Federal Marshalls escorted Gordon Wells and Kirk Logan by them to a waiting van. The prisoners were stopped by Florida's State Attorney General Nathan Randolph, who thrust State arrest warrants at both men. "Now it's the

State of Florida's turn," he said to Wynne. "They have violated some State of Florida laws, too. They'll be in prison so long with consecutive sentences there will never be another opportunity for fraud!"

## *EPILOGUE*

### *April, 1986*

THE DOORBELL RANG unexpectedly on Saturday morning as Wynne finished breakfast.

*Who could that be so early?* She quickly went to the door.

When she opened the door, an Air Force General, a middle-aged woman, and Chaplain Turner stood on the front porch. Jason stood behind them. Her thoughts flashed back to the similar visit she had received at dawn 14 years ago when the Squadron Group Commander and Chaplain brought her word that Michael was reported to be Missing In Action in Vietnam.

"Wynne," Chaplain Turner said. "This is General Arthur Ryan and his wife, Carole. General Ryan has some news about Michael. May we come in?"

Wynne recognized General Ryan as the Eglin AFB Commander. She knew that it could not be good news for the Base Commander, his wife, and a Chaplain to pay her a visit. *And why was Jason with them?*

"Yes...please come in," she said, her voice catching in her throat.

Jason embraced her and whispered, "General Ryan asked me to come, too."

"Mrs. Reardon," General Ryan said, "we have just received word that there has been positive identification through mitochondrial DNA testing of Major Reardon's remains in Vietnam. They are being returned to the United States for burial...I'm very sorry to have to be the bearer of such news, yet I expect it will bring closure at last."

Wynne sank to the sofa, steadying herself by clinging to Jason's hand. Jason sat down beside her, and held her tightly to him. Dry sobs shook her briefly.

"When will he be home?" Wynne asked as she regained her composure.

"Next Sunday...at Dover AFB. We will have an Honor Guard there."

"I want to be there, too," Wynne said, as steadily as she could manage.

"Certainly...we'll make the necessary arrangements for you and anyone you'd like to accompany you."

"I'll be glad to accompany you there, and perform the service later," Chaplain Turner offered.

"Thank you...I would like that. I would like for my son and daughter, my mother, Michael's mother, and Jason to be with me, too..."

"When and where would you like to have the services?" Chaplain Turner asked.

"At Arlington," Wynne said. "As soon as possible."

"We'll take care of it," General Ryan assured. "Will May 14th be satisfactory?"

"That will be fine," Wynne answered.

"This is the information we'll submit for the headstone," General Ryan said gently as he handed her a sheet of paper.

Wynne read the information that would appear on the white headstone beneath a cross.

*Medal of Honor*

*Major Michael J. Reardon*

*Florida*

*US Air Force*

*Vietnam*

*November 29, 1938*

*December 23, 1972*

"Thank you, General Ryan...Chaplain," Jason said as he saw the General, Mrs. Ryan, and the Chaplain to the door.

After the visitors left, Wynne called Stephen and Lauren. They agreed to meet her at Dover, and then go on to Arlington. She opened the chest of drawers, and took out the blue velvet box and Michael's last letter. She looked at the neat handwriting on the envelope – *Mrs. Michael Reardon.* She opened the envelope and read

*My darling...it's time to leave for another mission but there will be only a few more and I'll be home. I miss you more than words can say. Please kiss Stephen and Lauren for me and tell them that Dad will see them soon.*

*All my love,*
*Michael*

She put the letter back in the envelope, and placed it in the drawer. As she opened the blue velvet box and gently lifted out the Congressional Medal of Honor, the medal weighed heavily in her hand. She looked at the bronzed wreath, with a star hung from a baby blue ribbon, and thought how Michael's loss of life represented the true cost of freedom. Tears flowed down her face. She held the Medal momentarily against her damp cheek before putting it back in the box and placing it on top of his letter.

\*\*\*

*May 14, 1986*

THE SUN SHONE on the rolling slopes of Arlington National Cemetery as Major Michael Reardon's family and friends paid their last respects. The Military Band played *Amazing Grace* as the funeral cortege arrived at the burial site. Six paces behind the band, a Color Guard marched in precision with flags waving. Behind the Color Guard, a column of troops in ceremonial attire preceded Chaplain Turner. He walked 24 paces ahead of the caisson that was drawn by black Morgans and Shires, 16 hands high. When the cortege stopped by the burial site, gloved hands moved the casket from the caisson.

Wynne looked at the flag-draped casket as Chaplain Turner finished reading Michael's favorite verses from the Thirteenth Chapter of First Corinthians.

"...and now abide faith, hope, love, these three; but the greatest of these is love."

He concluded the service with a prayer, the words of the hymn *Abide with Me* which Wynne had requested:

*Abide with me: fast falls the Eventide;*

*The darkness deepens; Lord, with me abide!*

*When other helpers fail, and comforts flee,*

*Help of the helpless, O abide with me.  Amen*


Wynne flinched when the Honor Guard fired seven rifles in three volleys, and Air Force jets flew overhead in the missing man formation.

Chaplain Turner then walked to the edge of the grave with Wynne where she dropped a hand full of Florida sand on to the casket. As a lone bugler played *Taps*, the haunting sounds went to Wynne's very soul, and were reflected in the sadness in the eyes of all who stood with her. Tears welled in Stephen's and Lauren's eyes, as their mother returned to her chair next to them.

The Honor Guard folded the flag with exacting military prevision. The Air Force Captain, in charge of the Honor Guard, knelt before Wynne and handed the flag to her. He said, "On behalf of the President of the United States, the Department of the Air Force, and a grateful nation, we offer this flag for the faithful and dedicated service of Major Michael Reardon. God bless you and this family, and God bless the United States of America."

Jason held her arm tightly. Wynne looked across the Cemetery at the endless rows of plain white stones. They seemed to go on forever. Michael had finally come home and joined that number of dead heroes who gave their lives for their country. *He had made the world a better place to live -- she would always believe that.*

303

\*\*\*

**AFTER THE CEREMONY**, Stephen and Lauren cried with their mother and grandmothers and then hugged them good-bye.

"Are you ready to go?" Jason asked softly, his brown eyes riveted on her face.

"Could we stop by the Vietnam Veterans Memorial on the way to Andrews?"

Jason nodded and started to lead her away from the grave site. Chaplain Turner approached, and escorted them to the staff car. "Please call on me if there is anything further I can do," he said.

"You've been very helpful," Wynne replied. "We appreciate everything that you've done for us."

The Chaplain nodded and closed the car door.

As they crossed the Potomac River on Arlington Memorial Bridge, Wynne turned for one last glimpse at the National Cemetery. She watched until the green carpet and white headstones were no longer in sight.

"Please stop by the Vietnam Veterans Memorial," Jason said to the driver.

The young Lieutenant answered crisply, "Yes, Sir."

Wynne stood in front of the panel that held Michael's name. The sun cast a bright reflection off the black granite. She reached out and slowly traced each letter of his name with her finger - *MICHAEL J REARDON*. The radiant heat of the sun did little to dispel the coldness of the granite. As she traced the letter 'N", Jason reached out and closed his hand over hers. They turned and slowly walked away from the Memorial hand in hand.

***

ON THE FLIGHT back to Florida, Wynne reflected on the ceremony at Arlington. The occasion provided a finality to the loss of Michael that she had so desperately needed these many years. She remembered the comment her mother had made many years ago when they first learned of Michael's death: "Your life now is your Gallery." The Gallery had certainly been an important part of her life, but now she could embrace life completely.

It was no longer Mrs. Michael Reardon bound in her memories, but Wynne Reardon who turned to Jason and said, "...about the Gallery's Fifteenth Anniversary celebration next year. What do you think about having an invitational event with artists from the entire Southeastern United States? We could have a juried exhibit."

"I know which artist would get my vote," Jason said as he reached for her hand, his brown eyes expressing the same warmth she remembered from their first meeting. The sunlight reflected off the wing of the plane as though it were an affirmation of the promise her life's new beginning now held.

# *Author's Note*

Southeast Asia Map Source: CIA

THE VIETNAM WAR had its roots in French colonialism and World War II. The French pull-out of Vietnam after their defeat at Dien Bien Phou left the country divided between the Communist North and Western-backed South. The United States became increasingly involved as the North threatened to take over the South. In May of 1961, President Kennedy sent 400 military advisors to South Vietnam to train their soldiers. Regular United States' ground troops began arriving in 1965 under President Johnson's administration.

From 1965 to 1969 approximately 500,000 U.S. military personnel were involved in the war in an attempt to stop this communist aggression. Fifty-eight thousand Americans gave their lives. More than three million people, many Vietnamese citizens, also died between 1955 and 1975. The war ended in 1975 after communist forces seized control of Saigon. The country was then unified as the Socialist Republic of Vietnam the following year, with the name of the City of Saigon changed to Ho Chi Minh City.

# *About the Author*

## *Annie Laura Smith*

IS THE AUTHOR of numerous stories, articles, curriculum materials, and book reviews. Her middle-grade historical novel, *The Legacy of Bletchley Park*, was the first of her historical novels about World War II. *Will Paris Burn?*, *Saving da Vinci*, and *Alexandra's Secret* completed this historical series. *Twilight of Honor* moves forward in history and genre, providing a touching romance perspective to the war in Vietnam and its aftermath. Military wives and families can appreciate the turbulent emotions that follow with the loss of their loved one in times of war.

CPSIA information can be obtained at www.ICGtesting.com
Printed in the USA
LVOW08s0820160315

430631LV00035B/488/P